Working [illegible], she che[illegible]
of pictures until she found one that showed him
alone. She enlarged it.

It was him.

For an age she did nothing but hold her son so tightly she could feel the thrum of his little heart vibrate through his back.

How was it possible?

No wonder her five years of searching for Theo had been fruitless. She'd assumed living in the age of social media would make it an easy task, but had been foiled at every turn. It hadn't stopped her looking. She'd never given up hope of finding him.

But she might have searched for a thousand years and would still never have found him. The man she'd been seeking didn't exist.

It had all been a big fat lie.

Toby's father wasn't Theo Patakis, an engineer from Athens. He was Theseus Kalliakis. A prince.

You are formally invited to the Jubilee Gala of
His Majesty King Astraeus of Agon
as he commemorates 50 years on the throne.
Join us as we celebrate

The Kalliakis Crown

Royal by birth, ruthless by nature

This warrior nation's fierce Princes—
Talos, Theseus and Helios—each have their own
special gift to give their grandfather, the King.
But none of them is expecting the three women
who challenge their plans…and steal their hearts!

Discover the passion behind the palace doors…
watch as destinies are forged…and get swept up in a
torrent of emotion in this powerful new trilogy
by Michelle Smart!

Don't miss

Talos Claims His Virgin
December 2015

Theseus Discovers His Heir
January 2016

Helios Crowns His Mistress
February 2016

THESEUS DISCOVERS HIS HEIR

BY

MICHELLE SMART

Published in Great Britain 2016
by Mills & Boon, an imprint of Harlequin (UK) Limited,
Eton House, 18-24 Paradise Road, Richmond, Surrey, TW9 1SR

ISBN: 978-0-263-91579-2

Harlequin (UK) Limited's policy is to use papers that are natural, renewable and recyclable products and made from wood grown in sustainable forests. The logging and manufacturing processes conform to the legal environmental regulations of the country of origin.

Printed and bound in Spain
by CPI, Barcelona

Michelle Smart's love affair with books started when she was a baby, when she would cuddle them in her cot. A voracious reader of all genres, she found her love of romance established when she stumbled across her first Mills & Boon book at the age of twelve. She's been reading (and writing) them ever since. Michelle lives in Northamptonshire with her husband and two young Smarties.

Books by Michelle Smart

Mills & Boon Modern Romance

The Russian's Ultimatum
The Rings That Bind
The Perfect Cazorla Wife

The Kalliakis Crown

Talos Claims His Virgin

Society Weddings

The Greek's Pregnant Bride

The Irresistible Sicilians

What a Sicilian Husband Wants
The Sicilian's Unexpected Duty
Taming the Notorious Sicilian

Visit the Author Profile page at millsandboon.co.uk for more titles.

This book is dedicated to Jo aka 'Cat'.
Who has been there with me every step of the way.

CHAPTER ONE

JOANNE BROOKES COVERED her mouth to stifle a yawn and blinked rapidly to keep her eyes open. She was quite tempted to shove the thick pile of papers aside and have a nap at the small kitchen table, but she needed to read and digest as much as she could.

The floor creaked behind her and she turned to see Toby poke his head around the door of the tiny living space.

'What are you doing up, you little monkey?' she asked with a smile.

'I'm thirsty.'

'You've got water in your room.'

He gave an impish grin and padded over to her, his too-short pyjamas displaying his bare ankles. He hoisted himself up onto her lap and pressed his warm face into her neck.

'Do you *have* to go away?'

Wrapping her arms tightly around his skinny frame, Jo dropped a kiss in Toby's thick black hair. 'I wish I didn't.'

There was no point in explaining the finer details of why she had to leave for the island of Agon in the morning. Toby was four years old and any kind of rationalising normally went right over his head.

'Is ten days a long time?' he asked.

'It is to start with, but before you know it the time will have flown by and I'll be home.' She wouldn't lie to him, and could only dress her departure up into something bearable. Her stomach had been in knots all day, knitted so tightly she hadn't been able to eat a thing.

They'd only spent two nights apart since Toby's birth. Under normal circumstances she wouldn't even have considered going. It would have been a flat-out no.

'And just think what fun you'll have with Uncle Jonathan,' she added, injecting a huge dose of positivity into her voice.

'And Aunty Cathy?'

'Yes—and Aunty Cathy. And Lucy.'

Her brother and his wife lived in the local town with their year-old daughter. Toby adored them almost as much as they adored him. Even knowing that he would be in safe, loving hands, Jo hated the thought of being apart from him for such a long time.

But Giles, her boss, had been desperate. Fiona Samaras, their in-house biographer, who was working on the commemorative biography of the King of Agon, had been struck down with acute appendicitis. Jo was only a copywriter, but that didn't matter—she was the only other person who spoke Greek in the specialist publishing house she worked for. She wasn't completely fluent, but she knew enough to translate the research papers into English and make it readable.

If the biography wasn't complete by a week on Wednesday there wouldn't be time for it to be copy-edited and proofread and sent to the printers, who were waiting to print five thousand English language copies and courier them to the Agon palace in time for the gala.

The gala, exactly three weeks away, was to be a huge affair, celebrating fifty years of King Astraeus's reign. If they messed up the commemorative biography they would lose all the custom they'd gained from Agon's palace museum over the decades. Their reputation as a publisher of biographies and historical tomes would take a battering. Possibly a fatal one.

Jo loved her job—loved the work, loved the people. It might not be the exact career she'd dreamed of, but the support she'd received throughout the years had made up for it.

Giles had been so desperate for her to take on the job that he'd promised her a bonus and an extra fortnight's paid leave. How could she have said no? When everything was factored in, she hadn't been able to.

She'd been through the emotional mill enough to know she would survive this separation. It would rip her apart but she would get through it—and Toby would too. The past five years had taught her to be a survivor. And the money would be welcome. She would finally have enough to take Toby to Greece and begin the task of tracking down his father.

She wondered if she would have any time to begin her search whilst she was on Agon. Although Agon wasn't technically a Greek island, its closest neighbour was Crete and its people spoke Greek—which was why Jo had been the person her boss had turned to.

'We'll speak every day on the computer while I'm gone,' she said now, reiterating what she'd already told him a dozen times that day.

'And you'll get me a present?'

'I'll get you an *enormous* present,' she promised with a smile.

'The biggest present in the world?'

She tickled his sides. 'The biggest present I can stick in my suitcase.'

Toby giggled and tickled her neck. 'Can I see where you're going?'

'Sure.' She manoeuvred him around so that he faced her desk, pulled her laptop closer to them and clicked a button to bring it out of hibernation.

Having had only a day to prepare for the trip, she'd spent hours making arrangements for herself and Toby while trying to familiarise herself with the biography she needed to finish. She hadn't yet had the time to do any research on the island she was travelling to.

Keeping an arm around her son's waist to secure him on her lap, she typed *'Agon Royal Palace'* into the search bar and selected images.

Toby gasped when he saw what appeared and pressed a finger to the screen. 'You're going *there*?'

Jo was just as taken with the images, which showed an enormous sprawling palace that evoked romantic thoughts of hot Arabian nights.

'Yes, I am.'

'Will you have your own room?'

'I'll get an apartment in the palace.'

Until that moment she hadn't had time to consider the fact that she would be staying in a royal palace for ten nights. She moved her cursor down the screen slowly, looking for a better picture.

'Will you meet the King?'

She smiled at the eagerness in Toby's voice. She wondered how he would react if she were to tell him that she and Toby were distantly—*very* distantly—related to the British royal family. He'd probably spring to the ceiling with excitement.

'I'll be working for the King's grandson, who's a prince, but I might meet the King too. Shall I find a picture of him?'

She typed in *'King of Agon'* and hit the search button.

She supposed she should send Toby back to bed, but she really didn't want to—not when he was so warm and snuggly on her lap, and especially not when she knew he wouldn't be warm and snuggly on her lap again for another ten days.

The search revealed hundreds, if not thousands of pictures of the King. Scrolling through them, she thought how distinguished he looked. There were pictures of him with his late wife, Queen Rhea, who had died five years ago, others with his eldest grandson and heir, Helios, and one of King Astraeus standing with all three of his grandsons—one of whom must be Theseus, the Prince she would be directly reporting to…

She stared hard at the picture of the King and his grandsons and felt the hairs on her arms lifting. With a hand that suddenly seemed to be filled with lead, she enlarged the photo to fill the screen.

It couldn't be.

Making sure not to squash her son, she leaned forward and adjusted the screen so she could peer at it more closely. The picture was too grainy for her to see with any certainty.

It couldn't be...

'Are those men kings too?' Toby asked.

She couldn't speak, could only manage a quick shake of her head before she clicked on to another picture of the King with his grandsons.

This photo was of a much higher quality and had been taken from less distance.

Her head buzzed and burned, every pulse in her body hammering.

Working frantically, she clicked through dozens of pictures until she found one that showed him alone. She enlarged it.

It was him.

For an age she did nothing but hold her son so tightly she could feel the thrum of his little heart vibrating through his back.

How was it possible?

Two hours later she was still there on her laptop, searching through everything the internet had to offer about Prince Theseus Kalliakis. Somehow she'd managed to pull herself out of the cold stupor she'd slipped into at seeing Theo's face on the screen for long enough to tuck Toby back into bed and kiss him goodnight.

All that ran through her head now was crystal clarity.

No wonder her years of searching for Theo had been fruitless. She'd assumed that living in the age of social media would have made it an easy task, but she had been foiled at every turn. It hadn't stopped her looking. She'd never given up hope of finding him.

But she might have searched for a thousand years and would still never have found him. Because the man she'd been seeking didn't exist.

It had all been a big lie.

Toby's father wasn't Theo Patakis, an engineer from Athens. He was Theseus Kalliakis. A prince.

Prince Theseus Kalliakis stepped out of his office and into his private apartment just as his phone vibrated in his pocket. He dug it out and put it to his ear.

'She's on her way,' said Dimitris, his private secretary, without any preamble.

Theseus killed the call, strode into his bedroom and put the phone on his bureau.

He'd spent most of the day sleeping off the after-effects of the Royal Ball his older brother, Helios had hosted the night before, and catching up on reports relating to the various businesses he and his two brothers invested in under the Kalliakis Investment Company name. Now it was time to change out of his jeans and T-shirt.

He would greet Miss Brookes, then spend some time with his grandfather while she settled in. His grandfather's nurse had messaged him to say the King was having a good spell and Theseus was loath to miss spending private time with him when he was lucid.

Nikos, his right-hand man, had laid out a freshly pressed

suit for him. Theseus had heard tales of royalty from other nations actually being dressed by their personal staff, something that had always struck him as slightly ludicrous. He was a man. He dressed himself. His lips curved in amusement as he imagined Nikos's reaction should he request that the man do his shirt buttons up for him. All Nikos's respect would be gone in an instant. He would think Theseus had lost his testosterone.

Once dressed, he rubbed a little wax between his hands and worked it quickly into his hair, then added a splash of cologne. He was done.

Exiting his apartment, he headed down a flight of stairs and walked briskly along a long, narrow corridor lit up by tiny ceiling lights. After walking through three more corridors he cut through the palace kitchens, then through four more corridors, until he arrived at the stateroom where he would meet Fiona Samaras's replacement.

Murmured voices sounded from behind the open door. The replacement had clearly arrived—something that relieved him greatly.

His grandfather's illness had forced the brothers to bring the Jubilee Gala forward by three months. That had meant that the deadline for completing a biography of his grandfather—which Theseus had tasked himself with producing—had been brought forward too.

His relationship with his grandfather had never been easy. Theseus freely admitted he'd been a nightmare to raise. He'd thoroughly enjoyed the outdoor pursuits which had come with being a young Agon prince, but had openly despised the rest of it—the boundaries, the stuffy protocol and all the other constraints that came with his title.

His demand for a sabbatical and the consequences of his absence had caused a further rift between him and his grandfather that had never fully healed. He hoped the biography would go some way to mending that rift before his grandfather's frail body succumbed to the cancer eating at it.

Five years of exemplary behaviour did not make up for almost three decades of errant behaviour. This was his last chance to prove to his grandfather that the Kalliakis name *did* mean something to him.

But first the damn thing needed to be completed. The deadline was tight enough without Fiona's appendicitis derailing the project further.

Her replacement had better be up for the task. Giles had sworn she was perfect for it… Theseus had no choice but to trust his judgement.

Dimitris stood with his back to the door, talking to the woman Theseus assumed to be Despinis Brookes.

'You got back from the airport quickly,' he said as he stepped into the stateroom.

Dimitris turned around and straightened. 'Traffic was light, Your Highness.'

The woman behind him stepped forward. He moved towards her, his hand outstretched. 'It is a pleasure to meet you, Miss Brookes,' he said in English. 'Thank you for coming at such short notice.'

He would keep his doubts to himself. She would be under enough pressure to deliver without him adding to it. His job, from this point onwards, was as support vehicle. He would treat her as if she were one of the young men and women whose start-up businesses he and his brothers invested in.

His role in their company was officially finance director. Unofficially he saw himself as chief cheerleader—good cop to his younger brother Talos's bad cop—there to give encouragement and help those people realise their dreams in a way he could never realise his own. But woe betide them if they should lie to him or cheat him. The few who'd been foolish enough to do that had been taught a lesson they would never forget.

He wasn't a Kalliakis for nothing.

He waited for Miss Brookes to take his hand. Possibly she would curtsey. Many non-islanders did, although protocol did not insist on it unless it was an official function.

She didn't take his offered hand. Just stared at him with an expression he didn't quite understand but which made the hairs on his nape shoot up.

'Despinis?'

Possibly she was overwhelmed at meeting a prince? It happened…

In the hanging silence he looked at her properly, seeing things that he'd failed to notice in his hurry to be introduced and get down to business. The colour of her hair was familiar, a deep russet-red, like the colour of the autumn leaves he'd used to crunch through when he'd been at boarding school in England. It fell like an undulating wave over her shoulders and down her back, framing a pretty face with an English rose complexion, high cheekbones and generous bee-stung lips. Blue-grey eyes pierced him with a look of intense concentration…

He *knew* those eyes. He *knew* that hair. It wasn't a common colour, more like something from the artistic imagination of the old masters of the Renaissance than anything real. But it was those eyes that really cut him short. They too were an unusual shade—impossible to define, but evocative of early-morning skies before the sun had fully risen.

And as all these thoughts rushed through his mind she finally advanced her hand into his and spoke two words. The final two little syllables were delivered with a compacted tightness that sliced through him upon impact.

'Hello, *Theo*.'

He didn't recognise her.

Jo didn't know what she'd expected. A hundred scenarios had played out in her mind over the past twenty hours.

Not one of those scenarios had involved him not remembering her.

It was like rubbing salt in an open, festering wound.

Something flickered in his dark eyes, and then she caught the flare of recognition.

'Jo?'

As he spoke her name, the question strongly inflected in a rich, accented voice that sounded just as she imagined a creamy chocolate mousse would sound if it could talk, his long fingers wrapped around hers.

She nodded and bit into her bottom lip, which had gone decidedly wobbly. Her whole body suddenly felt very wobbly, as if her bones had turned into overcooked noodles.

His hand felt so *warm*.

It shouldn't feel warm. It should feel as cold as his lying heart.

And she shouldn't feel an overwhelming urge to burst into tears.

She wouldn't give him the satisfaction.

Straightening her spine, Jo tugged her hand out of his warm hold and resisted the impulse to wipe it on her skirt, to rid herself of a touch she had once yearned for.

'It's been a long time,' she said, deliberately keeping her tone cool, trying to turn her lips upwards into the semblance of a smile.

But how could you smile when your one and only lover, the man you'd spent five years searching for, the father of your child, didn't remember your face?

How could you force a smile when you'd spent five years searching for a lie?

Dimitris, the man who'd collected her from the airport and introduced himself as His Highness's private secretary, was watching their interaction with interest.

'Do you two know each other?'

'Despinis Brookes is an old acquaintance of mine,' said

Theo—or Theseus—or whatever his name was. 'We met when I was on my sabbatical.'

Oh, was *that* what he'd been doing on Illya? He'd been on a *sabbatical*?

And she was an *acquaintance*?

She supposed it was better than being described as one of his one-night stands.

And at least he hadn't had the temerity to call her an old friend.

'I saw a picture of you on the internet last night when I was researching your island,' she said, injecting brightness into her tone, giving no hint that she'd even *thought* of him during the intervening years. 'I thought it looked like you.'

She might not have much pride left after spending the last four years as a single mother, but she still had enough to be wounded and not to want to show it, especially as they had an audience. One thing motherhood had taught her was resilience. In fact it had taught her a lot of things, all of which had made her infinitely stronger than she'd been before.

Theseus appraised her openly, his dark brown eyes sweeping over her body. 'You look different to how I remember you.'

She knew she was physically memorable—it had been the bane of her childhood. Red hair and a weight problem had made her an easy target for bullies. Having Toby had been the kick she'd needed to shift the weight and keep it off. She would never be a stick-thin model but she'd grown to accept her curves.

She might be a few stone lighter, and her hair a few inches longer, but there was nothing else different about her.

'Your hair's shorter than I remember,' she said in return.

Five years ago Theseus's hair—so dark it appeared black—had been long, skimming his shoulders. Now it was short at the back, with the front sweeping across his forehead. On Illya she'd only ever seen him in shorts and the occasional T-shirt. Half the time he hadn't bothered with footwear. Now he wore a blue suit that looked as if it had cost more than her annual food bill, and shoes that shone so brightly he could probably see his reflection in them.

'You're looking good, though,' she added, nodding her head to add extra sincerity to her words.

What a shame that it was the truth.

Theo—or Theseus—or His Highness—wasn't the most handsome man she'd ever met, but there was something about him that captured the eye and kept you looking. A magnetism. He had a nose too bumpy to be considered ideal, deep-set dark brown eyes, a wide mouth that smiled easily and a strong jawline. This combined with his olive colouring, his height—which had to be a good foot over her own five foot four inches—and the wiry athleticism of his physique, gave the immediate impression of an unreconstructed 'man's man'.

Her awareness of him had been instant, from the second he'd stepped into Marin's Bar on Illya with a crowd of Scandinavian travellers hanging onto his every word. She'd taken one look at him and her heart had flipped over.

It had been a mad infatuation. Totally crazy. Irrational. All the things she'd reached the age of twenty-one without having once experienced had hit her with the force of a tsunami.

But now she was five years older, five years wiser, and she had a child to protect. Any infatuation had long gone.

Or so she'd thought.

But when he'd strode through the door of the stateroom the effect had been the same; as if the past five years had been erased.

'Different to all those years ago,' Theseus agreed, looking at his watch. 'I appreciate you've had a long day, but time is against us to get the biography complete. Let's take a walk to your apartment so you can freshen up and settle in. We can talk en route.'

He set off with Dimitris at his side.

Staring at his retreating back, it took Jo a few beats before she pulled herself together and scrambled after them.

Dull thuds pounded in her brain, bruising it, as the magnitude of her situation hit her.

For all these years she'd sworn to herself that she would find Toby's father and tell Theo about their son. She'd had no expectations of what would happen afterwards, but had known that at the very least she owed it to Toby to find him. She'd also thought she owed it to Theo to tell him he had a child.

But Theo didn't exist.

Whoever this man was, he was not the Theo Patakis she had once fallen in love with.

Theseus wasn't the father of her son; he was a stranger dressed in his skin.

CHAPTER TWO

'VISITORS TO THE palace often get lost, so I've arranged for a map to be left in your apartment,' Theseus said as they climbed a narrow set of stairs.

'A map? Seriously?' She would remain civil if it killed her. Which it probably would.

So many emotions were running through her she didn't know where one began and another ended.

He nodded, still steaming ahead. Her legs were working at a quick march to keep up with him as he turned into a dark corridor lit by tiny round ceiling lights.

'The palace has five hundred and seventy-three rooms.'

'Then I guess a map could come in handy,' she conceded, for want of anything else to say.

'There will not be time for you to explore the palace as you might like,' he said. 'However, we will do everything in our power to make your stay here as comfortable as it can be.'

'That's very kind of you,' she said, trying not to choke on her words.

'Are you up to speed with the project?'

'I read a good chunk of it on the plane,' she confirmed tightly.

As the deadline for the biography's completion was so tight, Fiona had been emailing each chapter as she'd finished it so they could be immediately edited. The editor working on it had spent the past six weeks or so with a distinctly frazzled look about her.

'Fiona has completed the bulk of the biography, but there is still another twenty-five years of my grandfather's life to be written about. I appreciate this must sound daunting, but you will find when you read through the research papers that there is much less complexity there than in his early years. Are you confident you can do this within the time constraints?'

'I wouldn't have accepted the job if I wasn't.' Fiona's editor, who Jo was now working with, had assured her that the last three decades of King Astraeus's life had been comparatively quiet after his early years.

But Jo had accepted the job before discovering who she would be working for and exactly who he was.

As she clung to the gold banister that lined the wall above a wide, cantilevered staircase that plunged them into another warren of passageways and corridors Jo remembered a trip to Buckingham Palace a few years back, and recalled how bright and airy it had seemed. The Agon Royal Palace matched Buckingham Palace for size, but it had a much darker, far greater gothic quality to it. It was a palace of secrets and intrigue.

Or was that just her rioting emotions making her read more into things? Her body had never felt so tight with nerves, while her brain had become a fog of hurt, anger, bewilderment and confusion.

'I don't remember you speaking Greek when we were on Illya,' he said, casting her a curious, almost suspicious glance that made her heart shudder.

'Everyone spoke English there,' she replied in faultless Greek, staring pointedly ahead and praying the dim light bouncing off the dark hardwood flooring would hide the burn suddenly ravaging her skin.

'That is true.' He came to a halt by a door at the beginning of another wide corridor. He turned the handle and pushed it open. 'This is your apartment for the duration of your stay. I'm going to visit my grandfather while you settle in—a maid will be with you shortly to unpack. Dimitris will come for you in an hour, and then we can sit down and discuss the project properly.'

And just like that he walked back down the corridor, leaving Jo staring at his retreating figure with a mixture of fury and incredibly lancing pain raging through her.

Was that *it*?

Was that all she was worth?

A woman he's once been intimate with suddenly reappears in his life and he doesn't even ask how she's been? Not the slightest hint of curiosity?

The only real reference to their past had been a comment about her speaking his language.

He'd sought *her* out back then. It had been *her* comfort he'd needed that night. And now she wasn't worth even a simple, *How are you?* or *How have you been?*

But then, she thought bitterly, it had all been a lie.

This man *wasn't* Theo.

A soft cough behind her reminded her that Dimitris was still there. He handed her a set of keys, wished her a pleasant stay and left her alone to explore her apartment.

Theseus blew air out of his mouth, nodding an automatic greeting to a passing servant.

Joanne Brookes.

Or, as he'd known her five years ago, Jo.

Now, *this* was a complication he hadn't anticipated. A most unwelcome complication.

Hers was a face from his past he'd never expected to see again, and certainly not in the palace, where a twist of fate had decreed she would spend ten days working closely with him.

She'd been there for him during the second worst night of his life, when he'd been forced to wait until the morning before he could leave the island of Illya and be taken to his seriously ill grandmother.

Jo had taken care of him. In more ways than one.

He remembered his surprise when he'd learned her age—twenty-one and fresh out of university. She'd looked much younger. She'd seemed younger than her years too.

He supposed that would now make her twenty-six. Strangely, she now seemed *older* than her years—not in her appearance, but in the way she held herself.

He experienced an awful sinking feeling as he remembered taking her number and making promises to call.

That sinking feeling deepened as he recalled his certainty after they'd had sex that she'd been a virgin.

She couldn't have been. She would have told you. Who would give her virginity to a man who was effectively a stranger?

Irrelevant, he told himself sharply.

Illya and his entire sabbatical had been a different life, and it was one he could never return to.

He was Prince Theseus Kalliakis, second in line to the Agon throne. *This* was his life. The fact that the new biographer was a face from the best time of his life meant nothing.

Theo Patakis was dead and all his memories had gone with him.

'*This* is where I'll be working?' Jo asked, hoping against hope that she was wrong.

She'd spent the past hour giving herself a good talking-to, reminding herself that anger didn't achieve anything. Whatever the next ten days had in store, holding on to her fury would do nothing but give her an ulcer. But then Dimitris had collected her from the small but well-appointed apartment she'd been given and taken her to Theseus's private offices, just across the corridor, and the fury had surged anew.

Her office was inside his private apartment and connected to his own office without so much as a doorway to separate them.

'This is the office Fiona used.' Theseus waved a hand at the sprawling fitted desks set against two walls to make an L shape. 'Nobody has touched it since she was admitted into hospital.'

'There's a spare room in my apartment that will make a perfectly functional office.'

'Fiona used that room when she first came here, but it proved problematic. The research papers I collated and my own notes only give the facts about my grandfather's life. I want this biography to show the man behind the throne. As I know you're aware, this project is going to be a surprise for my grandfather so any questions need to be directed to me. With the time constraints we're working under it is better for me to be on hand for whatever you need.'

'Whatever you feel is for the best.'

A black eyebrow rose at her tone but he nodded. 'Are you happy with your apartment?'

'It's perfectly adequate.'

Apart from being in the same wing as his.

How was she going to be able to concentrate on anything whilst being in such close proximity to him? Her stomach was a tangle of knots, her heart was all twisted and aching...and her head burned as her son's gorgeous little face swam before her eyes.

Toby deserved better than to have been conceived from a lie.

She knew nothing of this man other than the fact that he was a prince in a nation that revered its monarchy.

He was descended from warriors. He and his brothers had forged a reputation for being savvy businessmen. They'd also forged a reputation as ruthless. It didn't pay to cross any of them.

Theseus was powerful.

Until she got to know this man she couldn't even consider telling him about Toby. Not until she knew in her heart that he posed no threat to either of them.

'Only "adequate"?' he asked. 'If there is anything you feel is lacking, or anything you want, you need only say. I want your head free of trivia so you can concentrate on getting the biography completed on time.'

'I'll be sure to remember that.'

'Make sure you do. I have lived and breathed this project for many months. I will not have it derailed at the last hurdle.'

The threat in his voice was implicit.

Now she believed what Giles had told her when he'd begged her to take the job—if she failed Hamlin & Associates would lose their best client and likely their reputation in the process.

'I have ten days to complete it,' she replied tightly. 'I will make the deadline.'

'So long as we have an understanding, I suggest we don't waste another minute.'

Where was the charmer she remembered from Illya? The man who had made every woman's IQ plummet by just being in his presence?

She'd spent five years thinking about this man, four years living with a miniature version of him, and his presence in her life had been so great she'd been incapable of meeting anyone else. Once Toby had been born the secret dream she'd held of Theo—*Theseus*—calling her out of the blue with apologies that he'd lost his phone had died. As had the fantasy that she would tell him of their son and he would want to be involved in their lives.

Motherhood had brought out a pragmatism she hadn't known existed inside her. Until precisely one day ago she hadn't given up on her dream of finding him, but that wish had been purely for Toby's sake. All she'd wanted for herself was to find the courage to move on. She'd accepted she'd been nothing but a one-night stand for him and had found peace with that idea. Or so she'd thought.

Because somehow that was the worst part of it. Her body still reacted to him in exactly the way it had on Illya, with a sick, almost helpless longing. If he looked closely enough he'd be able to see her heart beating beneath the smart black top she wore.

His indifference towards her cut like a scalpel slicing through flesh.

He couldn't give a damn about her.

A swell of nausea rose in her and she knew she had to say something.

She couldn't spend the next ten days with such an enormous elephant in the room, even if she was the only one who could see it.

Heart hammering, she plunged in. 'Before I start work there's something we need to talk about.'

He contemplated her with narrowed eyes that showed nothing but indifference.

'I'm sorry,' she continued, swallowing back the fear, 'but if you want me focused I need to know why you let me and everyone else on Illya believe you were an engineer from Athens, travelling the world on the fruits of an inheritance, when you were really a prince from Agon.'

'It hardly matters—it was five years ago,' he said sardonically.

'You lied to me and every person you met on Illya.'

You lied to him too, her conscience reminded her, and she felt her cheeks flame as she recalled how her one lie had been the most grievous of all, a remembrance that knocked back a little of her fury and allowed her to gain a touch of perspective.

Her lie had been the catalyst for everything.

He contemplated her a little longer before leaning back against the wall and folding his arms across his chest.

'Let me tell you about life here on Agon,' he said thoughtfully. 'Outsiders struggle to understand but Agonites revere my family and have done so for over eight hundred years, ever since my ancestor Ares Patakis led a successful rebellion against the Venetian invaders.'

'Patakis?' she repeated. 'Is that where you got your assumed surname from?'

He nodded. 'My family have held the throne since then by overwhelming popular consent. With my family at the helm we've repelled any other nation foolish enough to think it can invade us. To prevent any despotic behaviour down the years my ancestors introduced a senate, for the people to have a voice, but still they look to us—their royal family—for leadership.'

Theseus's mind filtered to his father; the man who would have been king if a tragic car crash hadn't killed him prematurely along with his wife, Theseus's mother. Lelantos Kalliakis had been exactly the kind of man his ancestors had feared taking the throne and having absolute power. Yet, regardless of how debauched and narcissistic the man had been, the Agonites had mourned him as if a member of their own family had been killed. His sons, however, had only truly mourned their mother.

'We live in a goldfish bowl. The people here look up to my family. They revere us. Children on this island learn to read with picture books depicting tales of my ancestors. I wanted to meet *real* people and explore the world as a normal person would. I was curious as to how people would react to *me*—the man, not the Prince. So, yes, I lied to you about my true identity, just as I lied to everyone else. And if I had my time again I would tell the same lies, because they gave me a freedom I hadn't experienced before and will never experience again.'

The majority of this speech was one he had spouted numerous times, first to his grandfather, when he'd announced his intention to see the world, and then to his brothers, who'd seen his actions as a snub to the family name. After a lifetime of bad behaviour, when he'd effectively turned his back on protocol, taking off and renouncing the family name had been his most heinous crime of all. Even now he was still trying to make amends.

'If I hurt your feelings I apologise,' he added when she gave no response.

He didn't owe Jo anything, but neither did he want working with her to be a trial. There wasn't time to bring in anyone else to complete the biography and they'd already lost three precious days.

If getting her to soften towards him meant he had to eat a little humble pie, then so be it. He would accept it as penance for the greater good.

And, if he was being honest with himself, apologising went a little way towards easing the guilt that had been nibbling at his guts.

The only change in her demeanour was a deep breath and the clenching of her jaw. When she did speak it was through gritted teeth. 'I don't even know what to call you. Are you Theo or Theseus? Do I address you as Your Highness or Your Grace? Am I expected to curtsey to you?'

In the hazy realms of his memory lay the whisper of her shy smile and the memory of how her cheeks would turn as red as her hair whenever he spoke to her.

It was on the tip of his tongue to tell her to call him Theo. Being Theo had been the best time of his life…

No. He would not let those memories spring free. He'd locked them away for a reason and they could damn well stay there.

'You can call me Theseus. And no curtseying.'

Having people bow and scrape to him turned his stomach. All his life people had treated him with a reverence he'd done nothing to earn other than be born.

She nodded, biting her bottom lip. And what a gorgeous lip it was, he thought. How eminently kissable. He'd kissed that delectable mouth once…

'I ask you to put your bad feelings towards me to one side so we can work together effectively. Can you do that?'

After a long pause she inclined her head and her long red hair fell forward. She brushed it back and tucked it behind her ears.

'Do you remember the night those American travellers came into Marin's Bar?' she asked, in a voice that was definitely milder than the tone she'd used so far. 'You were with the Scandinavians on the big round table…'

He raised a shoulder in a shrug, unsure of what day she was speaking of. He'd hit it off with a group of Scandinavian travellers on the ferry from Split to Illya and had spent the majority of his fortnight on the unspoilt island in their company. Marin's Bar, which was two steps from the beach, had been the only place to go, but with its excellent beer, good food and a juke box that had pumped out classic tracks, it had engendered an easy, relaxed atmosphere.

Jo and her friends, whose names he didn't think he'd ever known, had always been on the periphery—there but in the background, rather like wallpaper.

'They were touching us up,' she reminded him.

'Ah.'

Now he remembered. The Americans—college graduates taking time out before joining the corporate world—had drunk far too much of the local liquor and had started harassing Jo and her friends. He remembered there had been something nasty about it, well beyond the usual banter one might expect in such an environment. He'd taken exception to it and had personally thrown the men out, then he had insisted Jo and her friends join him and his friends at their table.

And now her face did soften. Not completely—her cheeks were still clenched—but enough that her lips regained their plumpness. They almost curled into a smile.

'You stepped in to help us,' she said. 'Whether you were there as a lie or not, in that one aspect it doesn't matter. You did a good thing. I'll try to hold on to that whenever I feel like stabbing you. How does that sound?'

A bubble of laughter was propelled up his throat, startling him. He quickly recovered.

'I think that sounds like an excellent start.'

She rocked her head forward. 'Good.'

'But just in case you ever do feel like stabbing me I'll be sure to hide all the sharp objects.'

The plump lips finally formed into a smile and something dark flickered in her eyes, but was gone before he could analyse it.

'It's a deal. Now, if you'll excuse me, I believe this is the perfect cue for me to go back to my apartment and carry on reading Fiona's work.'

'Will you be ready to start writing in the morning?'

'That's very unlikely—I'm only two-thirds through and I still need to familiarise myself with the research papers. What I *can* promise is that I will have this biography completed by the deadline even if I have to kill myself doing it.'

She stepped out of the door, giving him a full view of her round bottom, perfectly displayed in the smart navy blue skirt she wore. What kind of underwear lay beneath…?

He blinked away the inappropriate thought.

Her underwear was none of his business.

But there was no denying the gauche young girl he'd known before had gone; in her place was a confident and, yes, a sexy woman.

It had been a long time since he'd considered a woman sexy or pondered over her underwear.

There was nothing wrong with admitting she had an allure about her. Thoughts and actions were different things. The days when he would already have been plotting her seduction were long gone. The Theseus who had put pleasure above duty had been banished.

The next woman he shared a bed with would be his wife.

CHAPTER THREE

JO GAZED AT the picture Toby proudly held up. Apparently it was a drawing of the two of them. It resembled a pair of colourful ants, one of which had been given long purple hair as his red felt-tip pen had run out.

'That's amazing,' she said, trying not to laugh, and inordinately proud of his attempt at a family portrait.

'Uncle Jon says he'll scab it for you.'

She stifled another giggle at his word for scan. At some point she knew she would have to tell him when he mangled words and mixed them up—like using alligator for escalator and Camilla for vanilla—but for the moment it was too cute. She'd start correcting him properly when he started school in five months' time.

She was dreading it—her baby growing up. They'd only been apart for one night so far, and this was already the second time they'd spoken via video-link. Thank God for technology.

She wondered how parents had handled time away from their children before video conferencing had been invented. A voice on the end of a phone was no substitute to seeing their faces as they spoke. Not that she would count her own parents in that equation.

She remembered going on a week-long school trip when she'd been eleven and calling home after three days only to have her mother say, 'Is there an emergency?'

'No, I—'

'Then I don't have the time to talk. It's feeding time.'

And that had been the end of *that* conversation. In the Brookes household the animals came first, Jonathan came second, with Jo and her father vying for last place.

'Sorry, sweet pea, but I have to go to work now,' Jo said, infusing her words with all the love her own mother had denied her.

He pulled a face. 'Already?'

'We'll talk again later.' Theseus would be expecting her at any minute.

'After lunch?'

'Tell Aunty Cathy we'll speak before you go to bed,' she promised, knowing full well that Cathy would be listening to their conversation and would make sure Toby was ready for her.

'Have you brought me a present yet, Mummy?' Toby asked, clearly doing everything he could to keep her talking for a little longer.

'I haven't been anywhere to get you one yet, you little monkey. Now, blow me a kiss and shoo before you're late for preschool.'

Toby did better than blow her a kiss. He put his face to the screen, puckered his lips and kissed it.

With her heart feeling as if it were about to expand out of her body, she pressed her fingers to her lips and then extended them to touch her screen. 'Love you.'

Before he could respond the connection was lost. No doubt he'd leaned on something he shouldn't have pressed when he'd leaned forward to kiss her.

Laughing whilst simultaneously wiping away a tear, Jo turned off her laptop.

She took three deep breaths to compose herself, then left her apartment, took four paces to the door opposite and entered her office, yawning widely.

'Late night?'

Theseus's voice startled her.

He stood in the archway that separated their offices, dressed in a navy suit and white shirt, without a tie.

She would never have imagined Theo in a suit, much less that he would look so unutterably gorgeous in it. On Illya he had lived in shorts, his golden chest with those defined muscles and that fine hair dusting over his pecs unashamedly on display.

But this man wasn't Theo, she reminded herself sharply. He was *nothing* like him. *This* man's lips seemed not to know how to smile. *This* man carried none of the warmth Theo had had in spades.

The only thing the two had in common was that same vivid masculinity. That vital presence. Her eyes would have been drawn to him even if she'd never known him as Theo.

'I stayed up to finish reading what Fiona had written,' she answered.

'Was that necessary?'

'I needed to find the rhythm of her work,' she explained evenly. 'I'll need to replicate it if I'm to make the transition seamless for the reader.'

'And are you ready to start writing now?'

'Not yet. I need to read through the research papers for the period of your grandfather's life I'm covering.'

He inclined his head and straightened. 'I shall leave you to it. I'll be back later if you find you have any questions for me.'

She forced a smile in acknowledgement, but the second she was alone she dropped her head onto the desk and closed her eyes.

Barely five minutes in his company and now not a single part of her felt right, as if being with him had caused her entire body to turn itself inside out.

She would have to find a way to manage it.

With grim determination she forced her attention to the piles of research papers before her.

The work Fiona had done on the biography had made for compelling reading.

King Astraeus had led a fascinating life, one filled with glory and honour. While many men of his nation had fought for the allies in the war—his brother among them—the then Prince Astraeus had led the defence of his own island. When a battalion of naval ships had approached the island with the intention to occupy it, Astraeus had led the counterattack. The fleet had been obliterated before it had reached the shore.

No other enemy ship had attempted to land on Agon since.

That would have been impressive on its own, but only the day before Astraeus had been given the news that his only brother had been killed in action.

This was Jo's son's heritage—a family that led from the front and who were all prepared to put their lives on the line to defend their home and their people.

A powerful family. And in it fitted Theseus—the father of her son.

The chapter Fiona had finished just before being taken ill detailed the death of Astraeus's only son and daughter-in-law in a tragic car crash twenty-six years ago. Theseus's parents. He'd been nine years old. So very young.

Her heart cracked a little to imagine what he must have gone through.

But that had been a long time ago, she reminded herself. Theseus the child had no bearing on Theseus the adult. She could not allow sympathy to lower her guard. Until she knew the real Theseus she couldn't afford to lower it for one second.

Theseus put his phone down. He could hear the soft rustle of papers being turned in the adjoining office.

When Fiona had worked on the biography he'd hardly

been aware of her. Other than the times when she would ask him questions, she might not have existed. Fiona using that office hadn't interrupted the flow of his own work.

As the financial figurehead of the Kalliakis Investment Company, and with his newer role of overseeing the palace accounts, which his grandfather had finally agreed to a year ago, he had plenty to keep his brain occupied.

In his childhood he'd dreamed of being an astronaut, of flying through the universe exploring new planets and solar systems. Astronauts had to be good with numbers, and he'd practised his arithmetic with a zeal that had astounded his tutor.

He could still remember one of the rare occasions when his father had come into Theseus's bedroom, mere months before he'd died. He'd looked at the star charts and pictures of rockets that had filled the walls and told him to rid his mind of such nonsense. A Kalliakis prince could *never* be an astronaut.

Even now Theseus would stare up at the night sky and be filled with longing.

He could have done it. He had the talent and the enthusiasm. He was fit, healthy and active.

But it could never be.

Now he used his talents, if not his enthusiasm, for financial reports. At least when he was going through the accounts he didn't have to put on a face and make small talk; didn't have to remember he was an ambassador for his family and his island.

So he kept himself busy. Too much time on his hands left his mind free to wander, to dream, to imagine *what if...?*

Today, though, the woman next door with hair like autumn leaves kept intruding. And she hadn't made so much as a peep of noise.

He couldn't get over how damned sexy she'd become. Even now, wearing nothing but charcoal three-quarter-length leggings, and a plain long-sleeved tunic-style black top that made her hair appear even more vibrant, she exuded a beguiling allure.

It had been a long time since he'd experienced such a primitive reaction to a woman.

Five years, to be exact.

His return to Agon from his sabbatical had been a turning point for him. Battling grief for his grandmother and ugly home truths from his grandfather, he'd known it was time to stop fighting. He would never be free. Sitting on the summit of Aconcagua in Argentina, the highest point in the Southern Hemisphere, was the closest he would ever get to the stars.

It had been time to accept his destiny.

He had decided he would curb his pleasure-seeking and throw himself into palace life. His grandfather had already been an old man. Helios had taken on many of his duties. It had been time for Theseus to take his share of them and relieve the burden.

He had been determined to prove to his grandfather that the Kalliakis name *did* mean something to him and had spent the years since his sabbatical doing exactly that—throwing himself into palace life and royal duties. In that time his appetite for sex had diminished to nothing, which suited him perfectly. Women who would usually turn his head had elicited minimal reaction. Neither his heart not his libido had been in it.

Now, for the first time in years, he felt the thrill of the chase coiling in his veins and cursed that such feelings should be unleashed.

Jo might be walking temptation, but there was no place in his life for desire. His next relationship would be with the woman he made his wife, even if he did intend on putting off the moment for as long as he could.

He stepped away from his desk and crossed the threshold into the adjoining office.

'How are you getting on?'

She didn't respond.

He was about to repeat his question but then saw she had earphones in.

She must have sensed his presence, for she turned her head and pulled them out.

'I will be leaving the palace shortly. Is there anything you need to talk to me about?'

'Not yet. I'm still going through the research papers and making notes on anything I feel could be relevant. As so many aspects are connected I think it will be best if we sit down and discuss it all when I'm done.'

'Will that not eat into your writing time?'

'It will make it easier—it means it will be solid in my head and I'll be in a position to work through it all without having to stop and interrupt you every five minutes. I'll probably still have further questions, but they will be far fewer this way.'

'I'm hosting a function for a delegation of French businessmen today, and I have a dinner at the US Embassy to attend this evening, but I can clear most of my diary for the next few days so I'll be available when you're ready.'

'That would be good, thank you,' she answered with a brief smile, her brilliant blue-grey eyes meeting his. She looked away, casting her gaze to her desk, then back up to him. 'Can I ask you something?'

'Of course.' So long as it wasn't about Illya. He refused to give headspace to memories from that time.

'Your grandfather's ill, isn't he?'

'How do you know that?' he asked, taken aback.

No one outside of the family circle and some select palace staff were supposed to know of his grandfather's cancer—which naturally meant the whole palace knew. However,

Theseus knew none of them would discuss it with anyone on the outside. Working in the Agon Royal Palace was considered an honour. To share confidential matters would be deemed treasonous.

'The publishing deadline was brought forward by three months and it was a tight enough deadline to begin with.' She shrugged, as if ashamed of her conclusion.

But it *was* the right conclusion.

It had occurred to Theseus, when the Jubilee Gala plans were first being discussed, that his grandfather had never seen his legacy in print. Usually Agon biographies were written after the reigning monarch had abdicated, then another would be written upon their death. As his grandfather had never abdicated that first book had never been written. He'd spent fifty years on the throne—the longest reign in three hundred years.

Suddenly he'd stumbled upon a tangible way to prove to his grandfather that he was proud of his heritage, proud to be a Kalliakis and, more than any of that, proud to call Astraeus his grandfather.

The more he'd immersed himself in his grandfather's life, the greater his pride had become. Astraeus Kalliakis was a true king. A man of honour. A man Theseus knew he should have emulated, not turned his back on for all those years.

This biography would be his personal tribute to him.

But then fate had stepped in. No sooner had he finished his research, and Fiona had flown over to the island to start writing it, than his grandfather had been given his diagnosis and everything had been brought forward by three months.

The Gala, the biography…everything was being rushed. Because now there lay the real danger that his grandfather wouldn't live long enough to see any of it.

The day drew nearer when he would have to say goodbye for the last time to the man who had raised him from the age of nine.

Theos, he would give his soul for a miracle.

Jo watched Theseus carefully. For a man usually so full of vitality he had a sudden stillness about him that she found unnerving.

Then his lips curved into a pensive smile and he nodded. 'Your intuition is right. My grandfather has cancer.'

'I'm sorry.'

'He's eighty-seven,' he said philosophically, but his eyes had dimmed.

'That doesn't make it any easier.' Jo had only known one of her grandparents: her paternal grandfather. She'd never seen much of him when she'd been growing up but she remembered how she'd always looked forward to his visits. When Granddad Bill came over her mother would bake even more cakes than usual and her father would drag himself out of the study where he spent his days drinking cheap whisky.

His death had saddened her but the distance between their lives had meant it had caused a dull ache rather than an acute pain.

It would be a thousand times harder for Theseus. The King was like a father to him.

He must be going through hell.

She remembered his despondency five years ago, when he'd learned his grandmother was dying. Whatever regrets Jo might have over that night, she would never regret being there for him.

Who amongst this palace of courtiers did he turn to for solace now? Who wrapped their arms around his neck and stroked his hair? Who tried to absorb his pain and give him comfort?

Because surely—*surely*—his pain that night had been real. Even if everything else had been a lie, that had been true.

Somewhere beneath the brooding façade Theseus was in agony. She would bet every penny she owned on it.

He tugged at his shirt collar as if it constricted him. 'The hardest thing to understand is why he didn't say anything sooner. He's known for a number of years that something was wrong but didn't say a word until the pain became intolerable. If he'd spoken sooner they might have been able to cure him, but…' He shrugged and closed his eyes. 'He left it too late. He's riddled with it.'

'Is he having any treatment?'

'Against the doctor's advice, yes.'

'They don't think it's a good idea?'

'His age and frailty are factors against it, but my grandfather is a stubborn old man who has never had to bow to the opinions of those he disagrees with—he is a king. He wants to live long enough to celebrate his jubilee and see Helios married. He has tasked the doctors with making that happen.'

Silence hung, forming a strangely intimate atmosphere that was broken by a knock on the door.

Theseus's eyes held hers for a beat longer before he called out, 'Come,' and a courtier entered with news that the delegation he was expecting had arrived.

Excusing himself, he disappeared, leaving Jo with nothing but her own confused thoughts for company.

She doubled over and laid her cheek on the desk, gazing at the closed door with unfocused eyes, trying to control the savage beat of her heart.

The King—her son's great-grandfather—was dying.

It brought it home as nothing else had that this family, however great and powerful they might be, were Toby's kin.

She gripped her head, felt a cramping pain catching in her belly. Her emotions were riding an unpredictable roller coaster. She might as well be blindfolded for all she knew of what the immediate future would bring.

But her conscience spoke loud and clear. Toby would start school in five months and the innocence with which he looked at the world would change. He knew he had a daddy who lived in Greece, but so far that was the extent of his knowledge and his curiosity. Soon the notion of a father wouldn't be some abstract thing but something concrete that all the other kids had and he would want too.

And didn't Theseus deserve to know that he was a father and be given the choice to be in Toby's life?

If only she had a crystal ball.

But no matter how much guilt she carried she could not forget that her overriding priority was her son. She would do *anything* to keep him safe, and if that meant keeping Theseus in the dark until she was certain his knowing could bring no harm to Toby, then that was what she must do.

Dictaphone and notepad in hand, Jo slipped through the archway into Theseus's office. After almost two days of going through the research papers she was ready for him.

He was on the phone. His desk—which, like her own, curved to cover two walls but was twice the size—was heaped with neat piles of files and folders. His three desktop computers were all switched on.

He nodded briefly in acknowledgement and raised a hand to indicate that he wouldn't be long.

While he continued his conversation she felt his eyes follow her as she stepped over to the window.

She loved gazing out over the palace grounds. No matter which window she looked out from the vista was always spectacular, with sprawling gardens that ran as far as the eye could see, lush with colourful spring flowers and verdant lawn, and the palace maze rising high in the distance.

When she looked back he was unabashedly studying her.

Prickles of self-consciousness swept through her. Flustered, she smoothed her sweater down over her stomach and forced her gaze back outside, scolding herself for reading anything into his contemplative study of her. Her thin cream sweater and faded blue jeans were hardly the height of fashion.

'What can I help you with?' he asked once he'd finished his call.

'I'm ready with my questions for you.'

'Ask away.'

'It'll probably take a couple of hours to go through them all,' she warned him, conscious of how busy he must be.

'My diary is clear. I'm at your disposal. Please, take a seat.' He pointed to the armchair in the corner of his office and put his computers into sleep mode.

Sinking into the armchair's cosy softness, she resisted the urge to tuck her feet under her bottom.

'Before we discuss anything, I want to say how sorry I was to read about your parents' accident.'

Their tragic car crash had changed the course of Agon's history. It was something Jo knew would reverberate through the rest of her work, and as much as she would have liked to steer away from it, knowing that to talk about it would bring back painful memories for him, it wasn't something she could avoid.

His gaze held hers before he brushed away a lock of hair that had fallen into his eyes.

'See,' he said quietly, emotion swirling in his brown eyes, 'I didn't lie to you about everything.'

She didn't answer, keeping her gaze on his and then wrenching her eyes away to look at her notebook, trying to keep her thoughts coherent.

When they'd sat in his cabin on Illya he'd swigged at his bottle of gin and told her how much his grandmother meant to him, that she'd been the one to whom he'd turned after the death of his parents. Jo's heart had broken when she'd known he would be returning home to say his final goodbye.

'Did you know when you left Illya that that would be it for Theo Patakis?' she asked.

'Yes.'

'And are you happy with your real life or were you happier as Theo?'

His demeanour didn't change but his eyes became steely. 'I don't think these questions have any relevance to my grandfather's biography.'

'I know.'

'I am a prince of Agon. My duty is to my family and my island.'

'But does it make you *happy*?' she persisted.

'Happiness is not quantifiable,' he answered shortly, looking away to press a button on one of the four landline telephones on his desk. 'I'll order refreshments.'

With the thread of their conversation dismissed, Jo pulled out a small table tucked next to her so it sat between them, and put her Dictaphone on it.

'Do you mind if I record our conversation rather than take notes?' she asked once he'd ordered coffee and cake.

'If that's what works for you, then by all means.'

She pressed 'record' and glanced again at her notes.

'Am I right in thinking your grandfather would have abdicated when your father reached the age of forty?'

'That is correct. Agon monarchs traditionally step down when their heir turns forty. When my parents died Helios became heir.'

'And Helios was ten at the time?'

'Yes.'

'So any thoughts of abdication and retirement had to be put to one side?'

'My father was an only child. My grandfather's only sibling died fighting in the war, so there was no one suitable to act as regent until Helios came of age.'

'What plans did your grandfather have for his retirement?'

A shadow crossed his face, lines forming on his forehead. 'He was going to take a back seat for my grandmother.'

'She was a violinist?'

'Yes. When they married she was already world-famous. My grandfather's coronation limited the scope of when and where she could perform, so she concentrated on composing music rather than performing, which was her first love.'

'So that was their plan? For her to start performing again?'

'She still performed, but only a couple of times a year at carefully arranged events. His abdication would have freed her and enabled her to tour the world—something my grandfather was fully behind. He was looking forward to travelling with her.'

'He'd travelled much of the world as a monarch,' she pointed out.

'Travelling as monarch is different. He was an ambassador for our island.' He smiled grimly. 'When a member of my family travels on royal business he has a retinue of staff and an itinerary that leaves no room for spontaneity. Every minute is accounted for.'

Jo tried to imagine the Theo she'd met five years ago, the carefree adrenaline addict with the infectious smile and an impulsive zest for life, living under such restrictions.

An image flashed into her mind of a fully mature lion trapped in a small cage.

'Is that why your grandfather agreed you could take a sabbatical from your duties at the palace and travel the world?'

'It wasn't a question of agreement,' he replied shortly.

When Theseus had decided to leave he'd discussed it with his grandfather as a matter of courtesy. He'd wanted his blessing but it hadn't been imperative. He would have gone anyway. He'd graduated from Sandhurst and, loving military life, had stayed on in the army for a few more years. But then he'd turned twenty-eight and his family's eyes had turned to him. He'd been expected to take his place in the palace, as a good prince was supposed to do…

It had felt as if a hook had been placed around his neck, tightening as the day had loomed ever closer.

He'd known that once he was in the palace permanently, any hope of freedom would be gone for ever. His childhood dream of becoming an astronaut had long been buried, but that yearning for freedom, the wish to see new horizons and control his own destiny without thinking of the impact on the palace, had still been so vivid he'd been able to taste it on his tongue.

He'd thought of his parents, dead at an age not much older than he was now, their lives snuffed out in the blink of an eye. Would they have lived that final day in the same way if they'd known it would be their last?

And so he'd made up his mind to leave before protocol engulfed him and to live his life as if each day really was his last.

He'd become Theo Patakis: the man he might have been if fate hadn't made him a prince.

CHAPTER FOUR

A STRANGE DISQUIET slipped through him. Theseus shrugged it off, and was thankful when a maid came into the office with their refreshments, placing a tray down on the table where Jo had put her Dictaphone.

He saw her gaze flitter to the *karidopita*, a walnut and spice cake.

'Have a slice.' He lifted the plate for her.

'No, thank you.' While she poured the coffee her gaze lingered on the cake.

'Are you sure?'

She pulled a face. 'I put on weight just looking at it.'

'One slice won't hurt.'

'If I have one slice I'll want the rest of it, and before we know it I'll be running to the kitchen and holding the chef to ransom until he's made me a fresh one.' She said it with laughter in her voice, but there was no disguising the longing on her face.

He was about to encourage her again—to his mind a little bit of everything never hurt anyone—when he remembered her as she'd been on Illya. She still had her luscious curves now, but there was no denying that she'd lost weight—perhaps a couple of stone if he were any judge. It seemed her weight loss was an ongoing battle.

Moving the plate to his desk and out of her eyeline, he settled back in his chair, cradling his coffee cup in his hands.

He didn't miss the quick smile of gratitude she threw his

way. It was a smile that made his stomach pull and a wave of something he couldn't distinguish race through him.

'We were discussing my grandfather's plans for abdication,' he prompted her, keen to steer them back to their conversation and focus his mind on the job at hand rather than on *her*.

She threw him another grateful smile and leaned forward to press 'record' on her Dictaphone again. The movement pulled her sweater down enough to give him the tiniest glimpse of her milky cleavage.

A stab of lust pierced him. Thoughts he'd done his damnedest to keep at bay pushed through.

She had skin like satin. Breasts that...

With resolve like steel he pushed the unbidden memory away.

He was not that man who put his own pleasure above everything else any more.

Holding on to his steely resolve and keeping his head together, he answered her many questions, one leading directly to another, all the while stopping his thoughts from straying any further into forbidden territory.

It was a hard thing to do when the mouth posing the questions was so sinfully kissable.

By the time she'd asked her last question Jo's lower back ached from sitting in the same position for so long—three hours, according to her watch. She got up to stretch her legs and went to stand at the window.

Discussing his grandfather's life had felt strangely intimate and she was relieved that it was over. The way Theseus had stared at her throughout…

His dark eyes had never left her face. And she hadn't been able to wrench her gaze from his.

'There's a load of schoolchildren in your garden,' she said, saying the first thing that popped into her mind as she tried desperately to break through the weird atmosphere that had shrunk the spacious office into a tight, claustrophobic room.

'They'll be here for the tour,' he murmured, coming to stand by her side. 'The palace museum and grounds only open at weekends in the off season, but we arrange private midweek tours for schools and other groups. From the first of May until the first of September the grounds, museum and some parts of the palace are open every day. You can't walk anywhere without tripping over a tourist.'

'Is it hard, opening your home to strangers?'

He gave a tight smile. 'This is a palace—not a home.'

'It's *your* home.'

'Our private quarters are off-limits to visitors, but look around you. Where can I go if I want to enjoy the sun in privacy? As soon as I step out of my apartment there are courtiers by my side—' He broke off and muttered what sounded like an oath.

Jo would have pressed him further, but her throat had closed up. Theseus's nearness, his heat and the warm, oaky scent she remembered so well were all there, igniting her senses… She clenched her fists, fighting her body and its yearning to press closer, to actually touch him.

A heavily fortified black four-by-four pulled to a stop below them.

A tall man, very similar in looks to Theseus, stepped out of the back, followed by a rake-thin woman with raven-black hair and enormous sunglasses.

'Is that Helios?' she asked, grabbing at the distraction.

'Yes. And that's Princess Catalina from the principality of Monte Cleure.' Theseus placed his enormous hands on the windowsill. 'Between you and me, he'll be announcing their engagement at the Gala.'

'That's quick. Didn't they only meet at the ball last Saturday?'

'Our families have been friends for decades. Catalina's brother went to boarding school with us.'

'They don't look like a couple in love.'

Jo wasn't an expert in body language, but the way they walked together—past the schoolchildren who had all stopped what they were doing to gape at them—reminded her of her parents, who walked as if even brushing against each other might give them a disease.

And as she thought this, Theseus's arm brushed lightly against hers.

Her lungs tightened.

She could *feel* him.

'Heirs to the Agon throne marry for duty, not love,' he said, his voice unusually hard.

She looked at him. He was gazing intently out of the window, his jaw set.

'It's the twenty-first century.'

'And protocol has been adapted. Helios is the first Agon heir free to choose his own bride.'

'Can he choose anyone?'

'Anyone of royal blood.'

'Freedom with caveats? How sad.'

'It is the way things work here. Change takes time.'

'I hope they at least like and respect each other.'

She wondered if her parents' marriage would have been different if her mother had ever respected her father. Would her father have resorted to the demon drink if her mother hadn't been so disparaging towards him?

'My brother would never have married someone he didn't respect.' A marriage without respect had to be just as bad as a marriage without love, if not worse.

'When will they marry?'

'As soon as it can be arranged. Hopefully before…'

He didn't need to finish his sentence. Jo knew what he meant.

Before his grandfather died.

The mood shifted, the atmosphere becoming even heavier.

'It will be a full state wedding,' he explained curtly. 'That usually takes a good six months to organise. Helios wants this one to be arranged in a maximum of two months.'

'That's asking a lot.'

He shrugged. 'Our staff are the best. It will be done.'

'Are you expected to marry too?'

'The spare to the heir must produce more spares,' he said scathingly. 'Once Helios is married I will have to find a suitable royal bride of my own.'

'And what do you consider "suitable"?' she asked.

Of course it was only the fact that Theseus marrying meant Toby would have a stepmother, and eventually half-siblings to contend with, that made it feel as if a knife had been plunged into her heart.

Theseus was a prince. Princes needed their princesses.

'Someone who understands that it will be a union within which to make children.'

She strove to keep her voice casual. 'Don't you want love?'

The look he cast her could have curdled milk. 'Absolutely not. Only fools marry for love.'

'That's very cynical.'

'You think? Well, my mother loved my father, and all she got for her trouble was endless infidelity. My grandparents loved each other, but when my grandmother died my grandfather aged a decade overnight. It's not the cancer that's killing him; it's his broken heart. Love causes misery and I want no part of it. I want a bride who understands what palace life entails and who I can respect. Nothing more.'

Jo swallowed the bile rising in her throat.

Her memories of this man were filled with such warmth that this coldness chilled her.

Where had that man gone?

She wanted to argue with him, to tell him that surely the sweetness of love overrode anything else, but what would she know about it? The only person who'd ever truly loved her was her son, and in all honesty he had no choice in the matter, just as she had no choice but to love her own cold mother. In Jo's experience filial love was as automatic as breathing. Parental love was not.

What if Theseus's disdain for love extended to his children? There was a cynicism to him that scared her.

She couldn't bring herself to ask. Instead she took a quick breath and said, 'Will Helios's children be sent to boarding school, like you and your brothers were?'

This was a question that had played on her mind since she'd realised all the Princes had been packed off to boarding school. If she told Theseus about Toby, and if he recognised him as his son, would he expect him to be sent away too?

That was *if* he recognised him as his son.

What if he demanded a DNA test? The thought made her shudder.

So many 'what ifs'.

If only she could see what the future held.

'Of course. It is the Kalliakis tradition.'

'Is it traditional to be sent away at *eight*?'

'Yes.'

'That's such a young age.' She thought again of Toby, who still struggled to put his own socks on. To imagine being separated from him for months on end… No, she couldn't do it. Being apart from him while she was here on Agon was hard enough.

'I agree. Too young.'

She swallowed back her relief. 'Did you find it hard, leaving your home and family?'

'You have no idea,' he said, his tone harsher than she'd ever heard it.

'Was it easier for you, having Helios there already when you went?'

He looked at her and paused for a moment. 'Harder. I was always being compared to him. I wanted to be judged in my own right.'

'So were you always rivals?'

'What makes you ask that?' The intensity of his stare grew.

She pulled a rueful face, knowing she was reaching dangerous territory. 'I've been putting two and two together again. I saw a press cutting about your grandparents' wedding anniversary party, where you punched him in the face.'

To her amazement he shook his head and burst into laughter.

The transformation took her breath away.

It was the first time she'd heard him laugh since she'd arrived at the palace, and the sound dived straight through her skin.

Almost lazily he reached out and pressed a finger to her lips. 'You are a very astute woman.'

It was the lightest of touches, but enough for all the breath in her lungs to rush out in a whoosh and for her heart, which was already hammering, to accelerate.

'Yes, we were rivals,' he murmured. 'Helios was always destined to be King. My destiny was to be the perfect Prince, tucked in his shadow. It was a destiny I fought against. I didn't want to be in his shadow. I wanted to be in the sun.'

His finger drifted away from her mouth and slid across her cheek, leaving flickers of heat following his trail. If he moved any closer he'd be able to feel the thundering of her heart…

He stepped closer. 'My childhood was a battle for attention and freedom.'

He was going to kiss her.

Her senses were filled with him; his scent, his heat, the masculine essence he carried so effortlessly and that every part of her sang to.

She mustn't give in to it. She mustn't.

She cleared her throat. 'Is that why you're the perfect Prince now? Are you making up for your behaviour then?' Judging by the press cuttings, his behaviour over these past few years had been exemplary.

He stiffened. The hazy mist that had appeared in his eyes cleared. He pulled his hand away from her face and stepped back, his regal skin slipping into place effortlessly.

Breathing heavily, Jo tried to collect her scattered thoughts, tried dispelling the tingles racing through her.

He'd been about to kiss her.

And she'd been about to kiss him right back.

She still wanted to. Her mouth *ached* to feel his warm, firm lips upon hers again.

She could feel the invisible mark his finger had left on her lips, had to clench her hands into fists to stop them tracing it.

'Yes, you *are* an astute woman.' Theseus had regained his composure. 'Now, unless you have further questions about my grandfather, I have work to do.'

'I'm done,' she said quietly, edging away from him, side-stepping into her own office, glad of the dismissal.

Only when she was completely alone did she place her fingers to her lips and trace the mark he'd made on her mouth.

Theseus stood in the adjoining archway and looked into Joanne's office, as he'd done numerous times since she'd arrived on his island.

There she sat, hunched over her computer, earphones in, seemingly oblivious to his pursuing eyes.

Any doubts he'd had about Hamlin & Associates sending a relative novice to take Fiona's place had gone. Unashamed of asking for help with translation when needed, Jo had finished four chapters in three days, passing them to him for approval before sending them to the Oxford office for editing. At the rate she was going she would beat the Wednesday deadline by a comfortable margin.

It wasn't only her speed and work ethic that impressed him, but also the quality of the chapters she'd produced. He was certain the reader wouldn't be able to spot the transition between the two biographers.

His grandfather was coming to life on the page in a way he'd never anticipated. He'd enjoyed Fiona's chapters, and had read them almost like a history lesson. But Jo had taken up the story from Theseus's own childhood. Reading her chapters was like seeing his own life through his grandfather's eyes, with events he'd lived through taking on greater significance.

His grandparents' fortieth wedding anniversary celebrations were vivid on the page. He could taste the food that had been served, hear the music of the Agon orchestra, see the dancing couples on the ballroom floor… And, although she'd wisely left it unwritten, he could see his fourteen-year-old self launching at fifteen-year-old Helios in full view of all the distinguished guests, breaking his nose.

He could see his brother's blood soaking into the royal purple sash, see his grandmother's horror and his grandfather's fury. He could still taste his own blood as Helios—never one to shy away from a fight like any good Agonite—had launched himself right back at him.

What he couldn't remember was *why* he'd done it.

He remembered hating the stupid penguin suits he and his brothers had been forced to wear, hating the forced small talk with boring old people, hating it that a president's daughter he'd taken a liking to had made a beeline for his older brother.

Everyone had made a beeline for Helios.

Helios lived under even greater restrictions than he did, but his brother had always taken it in his stride, acting as if going on a date with three burly men with guns accompanying him was natural and not something to resent.

Their rivalry had been immense.

He smiled as he recalled their younger brother, Talos, then only twelve, pulling them apart.

Theseus had been in disgrace for months and confined to the five-hundred-and-seventy-three-roomed palace over the long hot summer.

And then his smile dropped.

He'd ruined his grandparents' special day. He'd shamed them.

He had shamed them many times with his selfish behaviour. Royal military parades, state banquets—all the events the three young Princes had attended Theseus had treated with an indifference bordering on disdain. He'd wanted to be somewhere, *anywhere* else, and he hadn't cared who'd known it.

Reading about these events in the book, even with his churlish behaviour omitted, had brought it all back to him—everything he was fighting to atone for. It was the humanity Jo brought to both his grandparents on the page that made it all seem so vivid again.

Yes. His doubts about her ability had truly been expelled. He enjoyed working with her, their back and forth conversations, the flashes of shared humour. He especially liked the way she blushed when she caught him looking at her. She made his veins bubble and his skin tingle, long-dead sensations blazing back to life.

He found it fascinating to watch her work; her face scrunched with intensity, her fingers flying over the keys of her computer, completely in the zone. Sometimes she sensed his presence and would turn her head, colour creeping over her cheeks when she saw him…

She drove him crazy. It had become a constant battle to keep his hands to himself. He'd been so close to kissing her. *So close.* He'd breathed in her scent and every part of him had reacted.

And that was dangerous.

He was about to turn away and return to the safety of his own desk when her phone vibrated loudly next to her.

With her earphones still in, she grabbed it with her right hand and swiped the screen in an absent manner. Whoever had messaged her must have been deemed worthy, for she straightened, brought the phone close to her face and pressed the screen.

She gazed at whatever she'd received, brushing her fingers gently over it, before lifting the phone to her mouth and kissing it gently.

His stomach roiled.

He'd assumed she didn't have a lover. It was easy to tell if a woman was in love—there was a certain glow she carried. Jo didn't have that glow. But the way she'd pressed her lips to that phone…as if she'd been trying to breathe in the essence of whoever had sent that message to her…

It was a gesture that made his skin feel as if needles were being pricked into it.

He remembered the way those lips had once felt under his own mouth, the clumsy eagerness he'd found there. The innocence.

'Who was that?' he asked loudly, stepping into the room, his curiosity burning.

But of course she didn't hear him. By the time he'd tapped on her shoulder, making her almost jump out of her seat, the screen on her phone had gone black.

'Who was that?' he repeated, when she'd tugged the earphones out with trembling hands.

Dark colour stained her cheeks, her teeth bit into her full lips and her eyes were wide...*fearful*?

What on earth did she have to be frightened of?

Her throat moved before she answered. 'It's private.'

'Private?'

'Private,' she repeated more decisively. 'Did you want me for anything?'

'Yes.' He folded his arms across his chest and without even considering his words said, 'I'm taking you out for dinner tonight.'

If there had been fear in her eyes before, all that rang out of them now was confusion. 'Why?'

'You need a break. You haven't seen anything of my island.'

'I'm here to work—not sightsee.'

'You'll burn out if you don't take a break.' He needed a break too, time away from the palace and the reams of courtiers if only for a few hours.

He knew next to nothing of this woman who had once been a beacon of light for him on a long, cold night.

An evening out would do them both good.

Her brows furrowed. 'I thought Agon was closed on Sundays.'

He fixed her with the stare his brother Talos used to such great effect. 'Let me worry about finding somewhere to go. You need a break from this office. I want you ready for a night out by seven o'clock—and no arguments or I'll have you taken to the dungeons.'

Her eyes widened in surprise before she let out a bark of laughter.

He felt his own bubble of mirth rise up too, but smothered it. 'Seven o'clock,' he said, his voice brooking no argument.

'I haven't got anything to wear,' she said matter-of-factly, as if that clinched it. As if that would let her off the hook.

On impulse, he leaned down to place his face before hers, taking in the ringing blue-grey eyes. He caught a hint of a light, feminine scent and inhaled.

'Dress casually. And if suitable clothing is an issue I would suggest not wearing anything at all.'

Her cheeks turned so red they nearly matched the colour of her hair.

Pulling back, feeling lighter than he'd felt in years, he sauntered through to his office, pausing at the threshold to add, 'If you're not finished by five o'clock Nikos will escort you out of here. The office door will be locked until the morning. See you at seven.'

He walked into his apartment, his pulse thundering in his ears, and closed the door behind him.

What the *hell* was he playing at? A night out was one thing—but suggesting she go *naked*? That was inviting trouble. It was the kind of comment Theo would have made.

For five years his physical desires had been dormant. Being around beautiful women was a regular occurrence in his life, but not one of them had tempted him. None of them made him feel as if his veins had been injected with red-hot treacle the way being with Jo did.

None of them had propelled him to make an impulsive offer of a date. Well, give an *order* for a date.

No, *not* a date. Merely an evening away from the confines of the palace for them both.

Now his senses were straining to remember what she had looked like naked, but their night together was still a blur; a ghost that couldn't be seen.

Something told him it would be best for that memory to remain a ghost.

CHAPTER FIVE

A LOUD KNOCK on her apartment door announced Theseus's arrival.

Jo took a deep breath through her nose and pulled open the door, her heart thundering erratically.

And there he stood.

Tonight he'd forsaken the business attire he usually wore and donned a pair of slim-fitting dark blue jeans that hugged his long, muscular thighs, a light grey shirt unbuttoned at the neck and a fitted brown leather jacket that showed off the breadth of his chest to perfection.

All of that, coupled with his deep olive features and thick dark hair… He looked sexy. And dangerous. So dangerous she should close the door in his face and plead a headache.

He looked…

He looked like *Theo*.

He stepped over the threshold and stood before her, gazing down with a slow shake of his head. The look in his eyes threatened to send her pulses racing out of her skin.

She tried to swallow but her throat had dried up. Only once had she seen that look. Five years ago.

She'd thought he was beautiful. She hadn't been stupid; had known she'd had no chance with him. He'd been as unobtainable as the film stars she'd loved to watch so much. Even then he'd been a man surrounded by a legion of admirers, men and women who all hung on to his every word and laughed at his every joke. Men like him didn't notice girls like her apart from to make fun of them.

The last thing she'd expected—the very last thing—was for him to stand up for her. To protect her. That one action had turned her crush into something more, making her heart swell and attach itself to him.

Even then she hadn't been naïve enough to think her adoration would be reciprocated. The world didn't work like that. Gorgeous, fit Greeks didn't fall for plump, shy English girls. He could befriend her, but desire her? Impossible.

And then he'd turned up at the chalet she'd shared with her friends, bottle of gin in hand, hair in disarray and wildness in his eyes…

That look in his eyes when he'd first kissed her… That same look was in his eyes now. It was a look that pierced her skin and made her recall for the thousandth time their one night together.

That night…

Losing her virginity to a drunk, melancholic man had been something she could never have expected, but it was something she would never regret, and not just because that one time had created Toby.

Theseus had needed her that night. That hadn't been a lie. He'd lain on the bed with the back of his head resting against her breasts, swigging from the bottle of gin. She'd run her fingers through his hair and listened to him talk.

He'd told her about his brothers and their fierce competitiveness, the penknives they'd each been given at the age of ten by their grandfather and how they would spend hours finding inanimate objects to throw them at as target practice, how the loser would be subjected to knuckle-rubs.

And then—she had never figured out how or why—the atmosphere had changed and he'd stopped talking. His eyes had gazed into hers with an expression she had never seen before but which had acted like a magnet, pulling her to him.

The stars might not have shone and fireworks might

not have exploded but she hadn't needed them to. For a few precious moments she had belonged to him and he had belonged to her.

For one solitary night she had been needed and loved and wanted, and it had filled her romantic heart with hope and tenderness.

She couldn't bear to think it had *all* been a lie.

She'd stood in the shower an hour ago with anticipation thrumming through her and had known she had to tell him about Toby. She could not in all good conscience keep it from him any longer.

Theseus was arrogant, and often curt, but he was also generous and thoughtful. He was a powerful man, but she'd seen no sign of him abusing that power. He wasn't Theo, but there had been a couple of times when she'd sworn she'd glimpsed the man she'd fallen in love with five years before.

She would wait until the biography was complete. It meant everything to him. For all his talk about disavowing love, she knew he loved his grandfather just as he'd loved his grandmother.

A few more days—that was all it would take. Two days at the most. Then her job would be done and she could turn his life upside down with the truth.

All she had to do was smother the awful feeling of deception she carried everywhere.

She felt such guilt. Every minute with him was clouded by her total awareness of him and the knowledge that she was hiding something so monumental. She'd thought her heart might jump out of her ribcage earlier, when he had almost caught her looking at another picture Toby had drawn which Jonathan had scanned and emailed over to her.

And now her heart was beating just as frantically, but with a hugely different rhythm. Flames licked through her veins at the look in Theseus's eyes. It was as if he wanted nothing more than to eat her whole. As if her knee-length mint crêpe dress with its flared sleeves and her flat black sandals made up the sexiest outfit he'd ever seen on a woman.

The nervous excitement that had built in her stomach almost skipped up and out of her throat when he dived a hand around her neck and gathered her hair in a bunch.

Without breaking stride, he kicked the door shut behind him, moved his other hand to her cheek and brought his mouth down on hers.

If a body could spontaneously combust, then Jo's did. The lit flames became a blaze—a dark, fiery ache which deepened in her pelvis as his lips moved over hers, firm but gentle, seductive but checked. Firmly controlled. His tongue darted out, prising her lips apart so it could slide slowly inside and dance against her own. His fingers were making gentle kneading motions against her cheek.

Everything was pushed out of her mind, clearing it to only him; his hot, lightly coffee-scented breath, his warm strong fingers, the heat unfurling from him and moving through her aching body. Sensation threaded everywhere… right through to the soles of her feet and the delicate skin of her eyelids.

She gripped his jacket, then reached up to wind her arms around his neck, the tips of her fingers skimming the smooth skin and rubbing against the soft bristles running up from his nape.

Deepening the kiss, he dropped his hand from her cheek to snake it around her waist, breaching that final physical distance between them so she stood flush against him, lost to everything but the rush of his deeply sensuous assault.

And then he jerked away and the kiss was broken.

Ramming his hands into his jeans pockets, he closed his eyes and swore. 'I apologise,' he said, his jaw clenched, his breathing heavy. 'I never meant for that to happen.'

'Neither did I,' she said quietly. She looked away, not wanting him to see the enormous dollop of guilt she knew must be reflected in her eyes.

'You're driving me crazy,' he said, with such starkness her gaze flew back to him.

Hunger. That was what she saw. His hunger for her.

She was slipping into dangerous waters and had no idea how to navigate her way out, a task made harder by the fact that her body throbbed from head to toe. She knew if he were to touch her again she would respond with the same wantonness.

How could she have allowed him to kiss her when she was keeping such a huge secret from him? Even if he knew about Toby it would be madness to think anything could happen between them. In a few months he would be searching for a bride. A *royal* bride.

She was as far removed from his ideal of the perfect royal bride as possible.

He held her gaze a beat longer before striding to the door and yanking it open.

His eyes flashed as he said, 'I suggest we leave now, because if you keep looking at me like that, I will not be responsible for the consequences.'

Jo paused for far too long, desire waging war with common sense.

Common sense clinched the victory.

She held her breath as she slipped past him, then followed him in silence out into the clear spring evening.

Her lips still burned from his kiss.

When he'd made love to her on Illya he'd been drunk.

This time he'd kissed her when he was sober. He desired her.

It shouldn't have made a difference.

It made all the difference in the world.

* * *

That had been the journey from hell, Theseus thought as Nikos brought the car to a stop.

What had he been *thinking*, kissing her like that?

He *hadn't* been thinking. At least not with his brain.

It had been that expression in her eyes that had done it for him, that open, wide-eyed desire.

Theos, how could *any* man look into those eyes and not want to drown in them?

Sitting in the back of the car for twenty minutes with her so close had been tantamount to torture. They hadn't exchanged a word.

He ran through all the reasons why he couldn't allow anything to happen between them. Or he tried to.

He couldn't think of one good reason why he shouldn't make love to her when every ounce of his being burned for her touch…

Because Jo wants more than you can ever give.

His spine stiffened as he recalled the promise he'd made to her on Illya. The promise he'd broken. Try as he might to ignore it, the guilt ate at him.

Jo wasn't the type of woman to go in for casual flings. She just wasn't. He'd known that five years ago but had allowed his desire and the emotions that had racked him that dark night to take over.

He would not do it again, would not take advantage of a woman who needed more from a lover than a solitary night. He could never offer her anything more, especially not now, when marriage loomed ever closer.

He might desire her, but he would control it.

Whatever the night might bring.

Club Giroud was one of the best kept secrets on Agon, open twenty-four-seven and located in a deceptively shabby secluded stone building near the top of Agon's highest mountain. No casual passer-by would guess that inside, at any one time, were dozens of the world's richest people and a fleet of parked cars collectively worth millions of dollars.

The interior was an entirely different matter.

They were met at the door by the concierge, who'd been watching out for them. Puffed up with importance at one of the royal Princes paying the establishment a visit, the man led them through a cavernous golden-hued dining hall, filled with beautiful, thin, chic women and men of varying shapes and sizes, all of whom turned their heads to stare at them. The concierge took them past the sweeping staircase that led up to the club itself, and outside to the sprawling terrace.

'I am totally underdressed,' Jo hissed the moment the fawning concierge had left them alone. 'All those women look as if they've just come off a catwalk.'

'You look beautiful,' he said simply, his eyes taking in every inch of her. Again.

There was nothing wrong with looking. Nothing at all.

'And don't forget I'm a prince of this island. I could wear a sack and my guest a binliner and I'd still be treated like royalty.'

'You *are* royalty,' she said with a mock scowl, although her cheeks heightened with colour at his compliment.

'Exactly. My presence gives the place a certain cache. It's a secret club for the filthy rich—playboys and billionaires who moor their yachts in our harbour and like to dine and play somewhere elusive and exclusive.'

'You like to come here?' she asked doubtfully, as if she knew of his disdain for these people whose lives were consumed with money: how to make it and how to spend it.

'If I were to take you anywhere else our picture would be all over the press by morning.' He gave a rueful shrug.

'I can always take you to Talos's boxing gym, if you would prefer?'

She raised her pretty red-brown eyebrows.

'And here you get to see my island.'

'Do I?'

'If you look, you'll see this is the best view in the whole of Agon.'

He'd ensured she had the best seat at the table—one that looked out from the mountain over the villages and towns dotted in the distance, towards the palace in the thickets of trees on the adjacent mountain and the dark blue of the Mediterranean, where the sun blinked its last goodnight. In a couple of hours the moon would be high enough to illuminate the whole island. It was a sight he wanted her to see.

It gave him enormous satisfaction to see she hadn't paid the blindest bit of attention to the view. Since they'd been seated she'd only had eyes for *him*.

He pointed. 'Do you see that high, rocky mountain in the distance?'

She nodded.

'When we were teenagers, my brothers and I would have races to the top.'

'You were allowed?'

'Of course. Within the palace walls we were expected to behave like princes, but outside we were expected to be fighting fit.'

'And who would win?'

'Normally Talos. Helios and I were so intent on beating each other we always forgot what a mountain Talos was himself. We'd get to the top and find him already there.' He smiled at the memories.

Jo squinted as she took it all in, her features softening. She nodded in the direction of the palace. 'Is that the maze all lit up?'

'It is,' he confirmed. 'There must be a group doing

an evening tour—there are night lights embedded in the hedges to light the way for them.'

She gave a sigh of wonder. 'I bet that's a fabulous experience. Your maze is huge—much bigger than the one at Hampton Court Palace. I got lost in that on a school trip when I was twelve.'

Her delight at the recollection of being lost in a maze made her whole face light up, whilst the mention of the British palace sparked a memory of his own. 'Aren't you distantly related to *your* royal family?'

Surprise ringed her blue-grey eyes. 'How can you remember that?'

'I have an excellent memory.'

The truth was his memories of those last few days on Illya were becoming clearer. The hazy details were crystallising.

The night after he'd evicted those Americans from Marin's Bar for their ill-treatment of her, he'd gone back there with his Scandinavian friends and invited Jo and her friends to join them again. Conversation had turned to everyone having to say one interesting fact about themselves. Jo's had been that she was distantly related to the British royal family. She'd found it so amusing that she'd burst into laughter.

It had been the first time he'd heard or seen her laugh—usually she was so shy. Her whole face had lit up, just as it was doing now. It had been the first time he'd noticed what a pretty face she had. It had been such a transformation that his interest had been well and truly piqued. He'd spent the rest of the evening talking to her, enchanted by this shy young woman who, once she got going, became witty and talkative.

Talking to her had been like bathing in a clear, sun-drenched lake after months of soaking in the salty sea. He remembered how torn she'd looked when her friends had said they wanted to return to their chalet. How disappointed he'd been when she'd got up from the table and wished him goodnight.

The next day he'd tried to convince her to go surfing on the north side of the island with them all. Her friends had jumped at the chance but Jo had politely refused. She'd happily tagged along to watch, however, sitting on the beach and refusing to acknowledge his cajoling to come into the water.

Shortly after that he'd gone with his Scandinavian friends to a nearby uninhabited island for a couple of days of mountain climbing.

When they'd returned, the first thing he'd heard when he'd charged his phone had been Helios's message telling him to come home. Their grandmother had been taken seriously ill and wasn't expected to survive.

For the second time in his life he'd been lost. The first time had been the night their grandfather had flown to their English boarding school to tell him and Helios that their parents had been killed. Nothing could ever touch that night for pain, but he'd had his brother there, and for that one night his grandfather—who in that moment had been a true grandfather to them—had held his two grandsons close.

On Illya he'd been alone, and far from his family. He'd been on an island in the middle of the Adriatic Sea where the only means of transport had been the daily ferry.

He'd finished half a bottle of gin in his chalet alone, waiting until he'd figured everyone would be in bed before staggering outside, intending to sit on the beach.

There had been a light on in Jo's chalet.

Thinking back, he was surprised he'd known which chalet had been hers.

'According to my mother, her side of the family has a direct link to Queen Victoria via many marriages,' she said now, in that same amused tone he remembered from five years ago. 'I think I'm something like six-hundred-and-thirty-ninth in line to the throne.'

'Being that far up the chain you must have grown up in your own palace,' he teased, playing along with her irreverence.

'I grew up in an Oxfordshire manor house so old and draughty it would have been warmer sleeping in an igloo.'

'Rather like sleeping in a palace, then,' he observed with a grin.

She laughed, her eyes meeting his. 'Your palace is wonderful and has hot running water. My parents' house has a boiler so old my mother passes it off as an original feature. Saying that, the kennels and the stables always have decent heating.'

'Did you have a lot of pets?' He could just see her fussing over a small army of dogs.

She pulled a face. 'Not quite. My mother turned the old outhouses into an animal sanctuary. She'll take any animal in: cats, dogs, hedgehogs, horses—donkeys, even. Those she can't rehome, she keeps.'

'How many animals does she have?'

Her lips pursed as she thought. 'Anything up to fifty of them. If she runs out of space she brings them into the house.'

'That must have been magical for you as a child.'

She gave a shrug, her answer delayed by the waiter coming over with a jug of water and taking their order.

'So your mother runs an animal sanctuary—what does your father do?' he asked once they were alone again.

'He drinks.'

His hand paused on his glass.

'He's an alcoholic.'

'I'm sorry. Is he violent?' He thought again of the drunken American college students who'd been so abusive to Jo and her friends. Drink had a habit of making some people cruel.

'God, no. He's actually very placid. He just sits in his study all day, working his way through his whisky.'

'How does your mother cope?'

'By ignoring him.'

'Really?'

'She despises him,' Jo said flatly. 'As far as she's concerned, Dad spending his days pickling his liver is the best thing for him.'

His brow furrowed. 'That's harsh.'

'It's the truth. She thinks he's weak and foolish. Maybe she's right. He was a stockbroker, but he lost his job to the drink when I was a baby.'

'So how do they survive?' He couldn't imagine an animal sanctuary made much money.

'Mum's got a tiny trust fund, and she makes a little from donations to the sanctuary. She bakes a lot of cakes and sells them for high prices which our rich neighbours are happy to pay because they are utterly gorgeous.'

Not as gorgeous as the mouth doing the talking now, Theseus thought, noticing the faraway look in her eyes as she spoke of the cakes and remembering the longing she'd shown towards the *karidopita*.

'She sounds like a formidable woman,' he observed. His own mother had been the opposite of formidable.

Jo met his eyes. 'That's one way of describing her. She's very blunt with her opinions, and has no time for people she considers to be fools. Most people are scared of her and she knows it—she leaves the cakes in the front room with price tags on and no one has ever tried to short-change her or steal the money box.' She sighed. 'I'll say this much for her, though—she's dotty about the animals. It's only creatures who *don't* walk on four legs she has no interest in.'

The waiter returned with their wine and poured them each a glass.

'Do you still live with your parents?' Theseus asked after taking a sip of the mellow red liquid.

'I'm in Oxford itself now. It's easier to commute to work.'

That reminded him of something else she'd once told him. 'I thought you were moving to London?'

Her eyes widened. 'Gosh, your memory is on fire tonight.'

He flashed her a grin, wondering if he'd imagined the flicker of fright that had crossed over her face.

'So what happened to London?' he asked, watching as she reached for her glass of wine and noting the tremor in her hands. She reminded him of a jumpy cat walking on freshly tossed hot coals.

She looked out over the mountains. 'Life. But never mind about me—tell me about the business you run with your brothers. You invest in young start-up companies?'

He eyed her contemplatively. Yes. The jumpy cat analogy perfectly described her at this moment. Her discomfort had come on so suddenly it made him suspicious—until he reminded himself that he had no right to her secrets.

Jo was in his employ. The fact that they had once made love half a decade ago didn't mean he had the right to know everything about her.

Yet the more he was with her, the more he wanted to peel back every secret until she was stripped bare before him.

Did she have a lover? Instinct told him no—she wasn't the kind of woman to kiss a man if she was involved with someone else—but there was something going on with her…something she had no intention of sharing with him.

He took another sip of wine and pulled his errant thoughts back under control.

No more intimacies. This was *not* a seduction.

There would be no peeling back of anything; not secrets nor clothes.

So he told her about the business, keeping the conversation throughout their meal light and easy. By the time they'd finished their starters and main course—the pair of them having shared a generous *souvlaki* platter filled with marinated pork and chicken skewers, roasted vegetables, hot pitta, salads and tzatziki—and ordered coffee, she was as relaxed as he'd seen her on his island. So relaxed that when she declined dessert he held himself back from asking if her refusal of sweet foods was related to her mother's cakes.

And he'd relaxed too. With each sip of wine and every bite of food he'd felt the weight he lived with lift until it was just them. Two people who couldn't keep their eyes off each other.

Jo truly was glorious, with her autumn leaf hair thick around her shoulders, a lock falling around her cleavage. It would take no effort to lean across the table and slowly sweep it away, to trace his fingers over her satin skin…

'What?' she asked, one brow raised.

She must have read something in his expression, for her eyes suddenly widened and she grabbed her glass, holding it up like a shield.

Another memory flashed through his mind, of lying on his bed with her, his head cushioned on those wonderful breasts…

She'd been awake, book in hand, when he'd knocked on her chalet door. Her friends had been fast asleep.

When he'd swigged from his bottle of gin, shrugged his shoulders helplessly and said, 'I think I need a friend,' she'd stared at him, taking in his disarrayed state, then giving the most loving, sympathetic smile he'd ever been on the receiving end of.

'Come on,' she'd said, putting her book down and taking his hand to lead him back to his own chalet.

The bed being the only place to sit, she'd climbed on and sat against the headboard. He'd leaned into her. She'd laced her fingers through his hair and let him talk.

He still couldn't pinpoint when the mood had changed. He'd been drunk, but there had come a moment when he'd suddenly become aware of the erratic thud of her heart. He'd tilted his head to look at her and realised that while he'd been talking so self-indulgently his head had been resting on her comforting breasts. Breasts separated from him by nothing but a thin white T-shirt.

She'd worn no bra.

She'd smiled with those stunning blue-grey eyes and suddenly he'd known he could lose himself in them.

And just like that he'd been in a full state of arousal.

Forget comforting. She wasn't *comforting*. She was the sexiest creature on the planet and his desire for her in that moment had been the most concentrated, intense desire he'd ever experienced.

By the time he'd pulled her T-shirt off and wriggled out of his shorts he'd been ready to devour her. And he had done just that.

He'd fallen asleep as soon as it was over and had slept until she'd gently woken him to say that the ferry was approaching the island.

'That night in Illya,' he asked quietly, 'was I your first?'

'My first?'

'Lover.'

Understanding flashed over her and she covered her mouth with her hand.

'I was, wasn't I?'

She gave the barest of nods. 'I'm surprised you remember anything.'

Her face was suffused with colour. Abruptly she got to her feet, knocking into the table as she did so, spilling water from her glass.

'I need to use the ladies',' she said starkly.

He captured her wrist and stared at her, concerned. 'Are you okay?'

She nodded, but her eyes were wild. She tugged her hand free. 'I won't be long.'

Puzzled, he watched her flee inside.

No sooner had the door shut behind her than her phone began to vibrate and dance on the table.

CHAPTER SIX

JOANNE STARED AT her reflection in the lavish ladies' restroom—which was mercifully empty—and prayed for courage. Her hands were clammy, her skin burned and a heavy beat played in her head.

She had to tell him. Tonight. Forget waiting until the biography was finished. Things had gone too far to keep it hidden from him any longer. He was seducing her with his every word and every look.

She hadn't tasted a morsel of her food; could hardly remember what she'd had. Her senses had been too busy relishing the taste of his earlier kisses, the whispers of which still lay on her tongue and lips. She could still feel his huge hand warm on her wrist.

She inhaled deeply a couple of times before smoothing her hair and straightening her dress. She would drink her coffee, Nikos would drive them back to the palace and then, as soon as they were alone, she would tell Theseus the truth.

She slipped back into the club's restaurant and weaved her way through the tables of beautiful people, all looking at her with unabashed curiosity. She heard their whispers as she passed: this stranger in their midst was the guest of one of Agon's most eligible bachelors.

Avoiding Theseus's eyes, she took her seat and reached for her coffee, which had been brought in her absence.

Before she could plead a headache and ask if they could return to the palace, Theseus said, 'Jonathan called.'

Startled, she looked at him.

Impassively he handed over her phone. 'He called when you were in the bathroom.'

In her rush to escape from him and in the haze she'd fallen into she'd left her phone exposed on the table.

She swallowed, her heart immediately starting to hammer. 'Did you answer it?'

'Yes. I thought it might be important.' Curiosity rang from his dark eyes. And something else…something darker.

'What did he say?' she croaked, fighting the cold paralysis sweeping through her.

'Only that he was calling for a chat and that his scanner's broken, so he'll give you Toby's pictures when you get home.'

Jo felt the colour drain from her face at hearing him vocalise their son's name, the blood abandoning her head and leaving a cold fog in its place.

She hadn't told Jonathan or Cathy about finding Toby's father. She hadn't told anyone.

This was it. This was where the truth came out.

A pulse flickered in Theseus's jaw. 'So who are they?'

'Jonathan's my brother.'

'And Toby? Is he your nephew?'

It was a struggle to breathe. Her body didn't know what it was doing. She was hot and cold, thrumming and paralysed all at once.

Hot. Cold. Hot. Cold.

Fat tears welled in her eyes and spilled over before she had the chance to feel them form.

She took the biggest, most painful breath of her life.

'Toby is my son.'

The shock on his face was so stark it was clear that hadn't been the answer he'd expected. 'You have a *child*?'

She nodded and swiped the tears away, only to find them replaced with more.

He rubbed a hand through his hair and shook his head

in disbelief. 'I had no idea. You have a child…? How old is he?'

She wrapped her arms around herself and whispered, 'Four.'

His hand froze on his head. Slowly his gaze drifted to fix on her, then stilled, his expression like those on the statues of the fierce Minoan gods that lined the palace corridors.

Her stomach churned as she watched him make the connection.

An age passed before he showed any sign of movement other than the narrowing of his unblinking eyes. Slowly he brought his hand down from his head to grip his glass, which still had a little red wine in it. Without taking his eyes from her face he knocked it back, emptied the remnants of the bottle into the glass and knocked that back too.

He wiped his mouth with the back of his hand and got to his feet.

When he spoke, his words were laced with a snarl. 'Get up. We leave *now*.'

He was a father.

Those four words were all Theseus could focus on.

He'd known there was something in her life that was putting her on edge, but the truth was nothing like he'd imagined.

Jo had a child.

And *he* was the father.

He'd been on the brink of tossing away his vow of celibacy for a lying, deceptive…

Theos. He had a four-year-old boy out there—a child of his blood.

He hadn't needed to do more than rudimentary maths to know the child was his. One look at Jo's terrified, tearful face had confirmed the truth.

She'd denied him their son's existence.

She was sitting in the back of the stretch Mercedes alone while he rode in front with Nikos, who wisely hadn't uttered a word since they'd come out of Club Giroud. The partition was up. He couldn't bring himself to look at her.

His control hung by the tiniest of threads. There were so many emotions playing through him it was as if a tsunami had been set loose in his chest.

When they arrived back at the palace he got straight out of the car and yanked open the back door. 'Get out.'

Not looking at her, or waiting to see if she obeyed, Theseus unlocked the door to his private apartment and held it open for her.

As she walked past him he caught a whiff of that feminine scent that had been driving him crazy all week and his loathing ratcheted up another notch.

When they were alone in his apartment he slammed the door shut behind him and faced her.

'I was going to tell you,' she said, jumping in before he could say anything. She stood in the middle of the living area, her arms folded across her chest, her face as white as a freshly laundered sheet. 'I swear.'

'I'm sure you were,' he said with deliberate silkiness. 'Tell me, when *were* you planning on telling me? When my son was ten? When I was on my deathbed?'

'When the biography was finished.'

'You should have told me the minute you landed on Agon.' He gritted his teeth. 'You've had a whole week to tell me the truth. A whole week during which you have lied to me—so *many* lies. You sicken me.'

She blanched under the assault of his words, but straightened and kept her composure. 'I didn't know who you were until a week ago. I spent *five years* searching for an engineer called Theo, not a prince called Theseus. I thought *Theo* was Toby's father. When I realised, I had to do what was right for Toby. I had to protect him.'

He stopped his voice turning into a roar by the skin of his teeth. 'Protect him from me? His own father?'

'*Yes!* Look at you! You're a prince from a hugely powerful family with a reputation for ferocity. I didn't know *you*—I still don't. When I arrived here you were a stranger in Theo's skin. I had to be sure you posed no risk. To be honest, I'm still not sure. But I knew today that I had to tell you.'

'You *would* say that,' he said, fighting to hold on to his temper before it exploded out of him.

'It's the truth!' she cried. 'I know how much the biography means to you and I knew that to tell you before we'd finished it would derail you. I swear I was going to tell you as soon as it was done. I *swear*.'

'Stop with the swearing. Right now I don't know if I even care to believe your lies.' Something else occurred to him—something so profound he couldn't believe it had taken him so long to consider it. 'You said you were on the pill.'

She winced and gazed down at the floor. 'I lied,' she whispered. 'I'm so very sorry.'

'What?' He grabbed at his hair, then grazed his fingers down his face. 'How could you lie about such a thing?'

'I didn't mean to. I'm sorry. I wasn't thinking of the consequences,' she said, her voice muffled by her hair. 'I...'

But he didn't want to hear her excuses. There was only one thing he wanted from her, and that—*he*—was thousands of miles away.

'Where is my son?'

'At my brother's house.'

'Where?'

'In Oxford.'

'Where in Oxford?'

'At...' She stopped talking and raised her head to look at him. 'Why?'

'I'm going to send Nikos to collect him.'

She shook her head. 'He hasn't got a passport.'

'That is not a problem. The address?'

'You can't conjure a passport out of thin air,' she said with an air of desperation. 'There's a form that needs to be filled in, photos to be taken—it doesn't happen overnight.'

'I can make it happen overnight.'

'He's a British citizen. Only *I* can complete those forms because only *my* name is on his birth certificate.'

That cut him short.

Jo gave a hollow laugh. 'Yes, Theseus, your son has *my* name. Because his father promised he would be in touch, then probably deleted my number before the ferry had lost sight of Illya. You can condemn me for lying about being on the pill, but if you'd kept your promise I would have told you the minute the pregnancy test came back positive. You could have had your name put on that birth certificate alongside mine. If you'd told me the truth about who you were you would already *know* your son.'

That her words were mostly true did nothing to placate him. Did she really expect him to believe she would have told him? He didn't believe a word that came out of her pretty, lying mouth.

All he could think was that his son and heir had some sort of version of *'father unknown'* on his birth certificate. It was like another iced dagger being pushed through his frozen heart.

'Trust me,' he said coldly, 'I have ways of getting things done. My son will have my name and an Agon passport by morning.'

'You can't bring him here yet. He doesn't know you…'

'And it's past time that he did. Now, for the last time, give me the address.'

'I won't.' Jo refused to back down. However guilty she felt, and however understandably furious Theseus was, her first priority was her son. She would not have him frightened.

The pulse in his jaw throbbed. Her heart was beating to match it. He stalked over, crouched before her on his haunches and cupped her cheek.

'I want to see my son and you *will* facilitate this.'

He spoke the words with such quiet menace that acrid bile surged up her throat. She had never seen such naked rage before.

'Toby is not a toy,' she said, with as much steely control as she could muster, refusing to quail under the weight of his power and loathing. Strangely, his hold on her cheek, although firm, was surprisingly soothing. 'Your wish to see him does not trump his need to be and feel safe. I am not having a complete stranger whisk him away from everything he knows and loves. He's a *little boy*.'

His thumb brushed her cheekbone. 'A little boy who is my son. He belongs here in Agon.'

'Right now he belongs in England. You're a stranger to him—he needs time to get to know you before we even *think* about bringing him here.'

Was this really happening? Were they really having this discussion? She'd prepared herself for anger, or rejection, or if she was lucky faint promises of future contact—but not *this*.

'I have a four-year-old son I have never met. He *will* be brought here.'

She clamped her jaw together and forced air into her lungs. All she succeeded in doing was filling herself with his scent. She almost wished he would shout or throw something. Anything had to be better than this cool yet venomous reasoning.

'*I'm* his legal parent. I *want* you to be a part of his life, for Toby's sake, but I will not allow you to rush things.'

'How little you understand the workings of my country,'

he said, with what almost sounded like a purr—although there was nothing kitten-like about his tone. Its timbre and his stance were reminiscent of an alpha lion, getting ready to pounce. He stood up to his full height and headed to the apartment's front door. 'I have the means to bring him here and I *will* use them.'

Fresh panic clawed at her.

Where was he going?

'You *will* meet Toby, I promise. I know learning about him has come as a complete shock to you. You need time to process it—'

'Save me the psychobabble,' he cut in icily. 'All you need to think about is this: you will not be allowed to leave Agon until my son is brought here.'

Something cold and sharp pierced her chest.

'What are you talking about?' she whispered.

'I will put out an order that you're not to leave the palace without my express permission.' His lips curved but his brown eyes fired bullets at her. 'Even if you manage to escape you'll find yourself unable to leave the island. The minute you turn up at the airport or the harbour you'll be arrested.'

'You can't do that.' But the needles crawling over her skin reminded her that he could.

'You know the history of Agon as well as I do. My family may not rule the island alone any more but we do hold power. A lot of it. One phone call is all it will take.'

'Please, Theseus, think about what you're saying. I promise you will meet your son—but not like *this*.'

He turned the handle of the door. 'Do you think I will trust a single word you say when you have proved yourself to be a remorseless liar? I want my son here in his rightful home and I don't trust you to bring this about. If that means keeping you locked up until you come round to my way of thinking, then so be it.'

* * *

The clock's hands had barely turned to one a.m. when the apartment door was thrown open. Theseus strode in, a sheaf of papers in his hand.

After his threat to keep her locked up he'd left, disappearing into the maze that was the Agon Royal Palace.

She'd felt it best to let him go, hoping a little distance would give him time to calm down and see reason. She'd stayed where she was on his sofa, clutching at her hair, alternating between feeling frozen to her core one minute and burning hot the next.

And now, judging by the grim, dishevelled look on his handsome face and the wild, dangerous glint in his eye, she saw the past hour hadn't calmed him down at all.

Their time apart hadn't worked to restore her own equilibrium either, leaving her stuck in a strange form of paralysed limbo. It was almost a relief to have him charge back in.

'Fill this out and sign where the cross is,' he said without preamble, placing the papers on the bureau in the corner and stabbing the one on top with a finger.

'What is it?'

'A form acknowledging me as Toby's natural father. I need the relevant birth details from you. From this I will produce an Agon birth certificate. When you've completed this form I need you to sign this one for his passport.' He held up a pink sheet of paper. 'Nikos will fly to England and meet up with Agon's Ambassador. They will collect Toby, take his photo and produce the passport, then fly him here. Tell your brother to have Toby ready for midday.'

'Be reasonable,' she pleaded, knowing she was being backed into a corner she couldn't fight her way out of, but knowing that she *had* to fight—for Toby's sake if not her own. 'Toby will be *terrified* when two strangers turn up to spirit him away.'

'Not if he's properly prepared. You can call him first thing and tell him that two nice men are coming to bring him to you. Tell him to think of it as a great adventure.'

'If having Toby here means so much to you, then why aren't you going to get him yourself?' she asked, a sudden burst of bitterness running through her.

'Because my absence will be noted. I can't afford for anyone to know about him yet.'

'So you're going to bring him here and hide him away—is that what you're saying?'

'Only until after the Gala. That will give me almost a fortnight to get things organised and time to prepare my family—especially my grandfather—for the shock Toby's appearance will bring.'

'What are you going to do?' she demanded, spreading out her hands. 'Hide him in the dungeons? He looks *exactly* like you. Anyone will take one look at him and know he's of Kalliakis blood.'

Theseus felt his heart jolt at that information. He'd been so full of fire and fury that he hadn't yet considered what his son looked like. Or what his personality was like. *Theos*, did four-year-old boys even *have* personalities?

'I have a private villa on the outskirts of Resina,' he said, referring to Agon's capital. 'Toby will be taken there until after the Gala.'

'And what about me?' Her voice was high with anxiety. 'You can't keep him away from me. That would be beyond cruel.'

His lips curved into a sneer but he shook his head. 'Do not hold me to your own low standards. You will be taken there in the morning to wait for him.'

Not even in the darkest recess of his mind had he entertained the thought of keeping them apart—not even before he'd spoken to Dimitris and been given the hard facts about what having a child here would mean…not just for him but for Jo too.

For a moment his throat thickened as he saw the despair in her eyes.

She'd lied to him about being on the pill, he reminded himself angrily, whilst images of leaving Illya rained down in his mind.

He'd stood at the back of the ferry, staring at the woman who had helped him through one of the worst nights of his life. Jo had sat on the beach, hugging her legs and watching him leave. He'd kissed her goodbye before boarding, had tasted her sweetness for what he had thought would be the last time.

Why had he strung her along as he had? He'd never made false promises to a woman before. He'd known even as he'd stored her number in his phone that he would never call her. He'd never done that to a woman before. If he had no intention of calling, he never pretended that he would.

But she had *really* lied to him. He might have broken a minor promise to call but she had lied about being on the pill. If she hadn't told such a wicked lie…

He wouldn't have a son.

She'd hit a nerve when she'd asked why he wasn't going to collect him personally. *Theos*, he wanted to. If he had superhuman powers he would have already flown to him. And yet…

Trepidation had taken root.

He wasn't ready for this—wasn't ready to be an instant father. These few hours while his son was being brought to him would allow him to prepare himself and get his villa made suitable for a small boy.

'I'll give you twenty minutes to get the paperwork complete,' he said.

He'd left Dimitris in the palace library, researching constitutional matters, and he needed to check in with him. He could also do without Jo's accusatory stare following his every move. She had no right to look at him as if *he* were the bad guy.

If she thought things were bad for her now, she was in for a nasty shock when he told her the rest of it.

CHAPTER SEVEN

JO HAD LONG given up trying to sleep.

It had been three hours since she'd completed those forms. She'd left them on Theseus's bureau and returned to her own apartment, locking the door behind her.

She wanted to be alone, was too mentally exhausted to cope with anything else.

Padding over to the kitchen, she poured herself a glass of water and then rummaged in her handbag for some headache tablets. Just as she popped them into her mouth there was a soft rap on the door, followed by the sound of the handle being turned.

She swallowed the tablets down, more pathetic tears swimming in her eyes. It could only be Theseus.

She didn't want to see him. Not right now, when she was so angry and heartsick that she could punch him in the face. She ignored the knock.

Her numb shock had gone…had been replaced with a burning anger that he could be so cruel. Whatever wrong she'd done—and she'd always known what a terrible wrong it was—this was infinitely worse.

All those years of searching, all those years of raising her child as a single parent, and he thought he could sweep in and turn it all upside down with no consideration for Toby's emotional state.

And there was nothing she could do about it.

Every scratch of the pen on those forms had felt like a scratch on her heart.

But what choice had she had but to sign them? Theseus was fully prepared to keep her a prisoner until Toby was brought to him. She'd seen the threat in his eyes.

What this meant for her future she didn't know. His power was too much for her to fight—more than she could ever have appreciated. She was fighting from a power base of zero.

Her head pounded. And her eyes… They'd never felt so gritty—not even when she'd spent a whole day sobbing in fear over how her mother would react to her unexpected pregnancy. The fact that her mother's only comment had been, 'For God's sake, girl, I thought you had more sense than that,' had been rather anticlimactic after all the angst she'd put herself through.

She should have known her mother wouldn't be angry. For her to be angry would mean she cared, and if there was one thing Joanne had grown up knowing it was that her mother didn't care. Harriet Brookes had done her duty. She had fed her and clothed her. But that was the extent of any mothering she'd extended towards her daughter.

Even when Jo had spent a month in hospital whilst pregnant her mother had paid only one visit, and that had been to drive her back to the frigid shell she called a home.

At least her father had shown some kindness—but she'd had to catch him at the right time if she'd wanted any coherence from him, considering he started drinking in the morning and was generally comatose in the chair in his study by mid-afternoon.

Her poor father… That weak-willed, spineless man, who'd realised too late that the pretty young woman he'd impregnated and been forced to marry was far too strong for him. He'd once said, intoxicated over Sunday dinner, that she'd emasculated him. Her mother had replied in her usual no-nonsense manner that one needed balls to begin with in order to be emasculated.

Jo had not understood why they stayed together—and had *never* understood how they'd come to make *her*.

She knew she must get some sleep. Even if she only managed a couple of hours that would be better than nothing at all.

As she was about to climb back into the huge four-poster bed she froze when she heard the click of a door being unlocked, followed by a creak.

Slowly she turned her head to look at the door adjacent to her dressing room. She'd never been able to open it and had wondered a couple of times what lay on the other side. Now she stared as it opened, too frozen with fear to move.

Fight or flight? At that moment she wasn't capable of either option.

And then Theseus stepped over the threshold, allowing her to expel the breath she'd been holding.

He looked haggard, as if the events of the night had caused him to unravel.

'You scared the life out of me!' she said, on the verge of tears with shock. Her heart had been kick-started and was now pumping at the rate of knots. 'Where did you come from?'

'You didn't answer my knock so I came through the hidden passageway connecting your apartment with mine.' He pushed the door shut with his back and folded his arms. 'We need to talk.'

'It's four o'clock in the morning.' And she was wearing nothing but an old T-shirt that only just skimmed her fortunately covered bottom.

'And you're managing to sleep as well as I am.' His eyes flickered over her, taking in her attire. 'Nikos is on his way to England. There's a helicopter on standby to fly him and the ambassador to Oxford,' he added.

Jo gnawed at her lip and tried to fight the fresh tide of panic she felt as she did the maths. With the time difference between Agon and the UK, Nikos and the ambassador would easily make it to Toby by midday—just as Theseus had promised.

'I think it would be best if I meet him at the airport.' She mentally prepared herself for another fight she knew she was in no position to win.

To her surprise he gave a sharp nod of agreement. 'I'll get that arranged.'

'And we'll go straight to your villa?' she clarified.

'Yes.'

She chose her next words with care. Theseus might have calmed down, but she was aware that his temper was currently as flammable as dry kindling. 'I know you want us to stay until the Gala, and then introduce Toby to your family, but I need to know how long you'll want us to stay afterwards so I can make arrangements with work.'

At that moment she couldn't think about the biography and the work that still needed to be done to finish it.

When Theseus didn't answer, and simply stared at her with an unfathomable expression on his handsome face, alarm bells began to chime softly, reverberating through her stomach.

'How long do you envisage us staying on Agon for?' she asked again, more forcefully.

He rubbed the back of his neck. 'Dimitris and I have been refreshing our memories of Agon laws…'

'What's that got to do with how long Toby and I stay?'

'Everything.'

The alarm bells in her stomach upped their tempo, clanging loudly enough that they seemed to echo through her skin.

The silence thickened, closing in.

'You'll be staying on Agon indefinitely.'

'What are you talking about?'

'The only way Toby can be my heir is if we marry.'

Jo felt her jaw go slack. 'You have *got* to be joking.'

'I wish I was.' Theseus closed his eyes, then snapped them open to focus on her. 'Agon law states clearly that only legitimate heirs of the royal family can be recognised and allowed to inherit.'

'I don't understand...' she whispered, although the implications were already rushing through her.

'The law was created two hundred years ago, when the eldest of King Helios the Second's illegitimate children fought with his lawful heir for the right to take the throne. To prevent such a situation happening again it was explicitly spelt out in the constitution that only legitimate heirs can be recognised.'

'But Toby wasn't born in wedlock, so he'll be illegitimate regardless.'

'Our marriage will legitimise him. There is nothing in the constitution that states that the child must have been conceived or born in wedlock—only that they must be a child of a lawful marriage.'

Her hands fluttered to her throat. Her head shook slowly from left to right as she tried to take in exactly what he was saying. 'We can't marry. The idea is just...stupid.'

'Do you think I *want* to marry you?' he said harshly. 'It's the only way I can claim Toby as my own and give him the protection of the Kalliakis name.'

'He doesn't need protection. We live in Middle England—not a war zone.'

'The minute it's made public that I have a son he'll be a target for kidnappers the world over. But that's missing the point, which is that Toby is my son and deserves to be recognised as such. He deserves to be allowed to inherit my personal wealth.'

'What would you do if you were already married?' she challenged. 'Because you surely couldn't marry me then? Unless bigamy is legal on Agon?'

'We are not in that situation, so that's irrelevant. Let me put this in simple terms for you. You and I will marry as soon as we can. If you refuse you will be escorted—alone—off Agon and never allowed to return.'

'You wouldn't…' She shook her head, swallowing back her fury and distress as the full weight of his threat hit her like a brick.

His nostrils flared and he eased himself away from the door. 'Try me. If you refuse to marry me Toby will be raised on Agon without you. He will know the reason he's not recognised as a member of his own family and is unable to be my heir is because of his mother's selfishness.'

The room swam. 'Would you really stoop so low as to keep us apart and twist his mind against me?'

He raised a strong shoulder and sauntered to stand before her, where she still stood rooted to the spot beside the bed. 'Whatever I tell him would be nothing compared to the conclusions he would draw on his own. Now, do I have your agreement?'

She backed away lest she give in to her fingers' need to slap him. She wasn't being selfish. *She wasn't.* What Theseus demanded of her was unconscionable.

A thought raced through her, which she grasped and clung on to. 'You *can't* marry me—you have to marry a princess. Remember? You told me that yourself.'

'No, I have to marry someone with royal blood—which you have.'

'But my blood is so diluted it's weaker than supermarket own-brand blackcurrant squash!' She clung on to the thought desperately, too scared to let go of this last glimmer of hope. 'My family don't have titles or acres of land. There's not a lord or a viscount in sight!'

'It's enough to satisfy the constitution. It would be different if Helios was in my position—*he* is expected to marry a princess, or someone of equal heritage. Now, for the last time, do I have your agreement?'

With her stomach curdling and her skin feeling so tight she could feel her bones pushing through the flesh, Jo blinked frantically to keep her focus, to maintain some measure of control.

There was no way out. No other avenue to take. Theseus had thought of everything and had an answer to everything.

But she wouldn't let him have it all his own way.

'Seeing as I have no choice, I'll marry you. But only for long enough to satisfy whatever draconian law your ridiculous island insists on before we can divorce.'

He shook his head, his mouth twisting into a rueful grimace. 'It is illegal for members of the Agon royal family to divorce.'

'That's not possible.' Coldness like nothing she'd experienced before crept through her bones.

'The constitution—'

But she cut him off before he could say another word. All the fear and anger that had been brewing within her converged to the point of explosion and she launched herself at him, pushing him onto the bed, her fists striking his chest.

'Your constitution can take a running jump, for all I care, and so can you,' she raged. 'I'm *not* giving up my entire life for you.'

Theseus had her hands pinned and her body trapped beneath him before she could take another breath.

'You're not sacrificing your life for me but for Toby,' he snarled, his breath hot on her face.

She could sense his fury, matching hers in its strength. Her blood was pumping so fast it heated her veins to boiling point.

She bucked beneath him, kicking her legs out wildly. 'Toby is the happiest child in the world! I've sacrificed *everything* to love and care for him and now you want me to throw our lives away just so you can lay claim to him, as if he's some possession and not a flesh and blood boy.'

'He's a prince of Agon and he deserves the protection and everything else that comes with the title.'

Theseus trapped her kicking legs with a thigh. *Theos*, the shy wallflower he'd met in Illya had more fight in her than he'd ever imagined. Even though his emotions were as intense as he'd ever known them, his body could not help but react to her.

'If *you're* a reflection of the way a prince of Agon turns out then I'd much rather he stays a commoner,' she spat back.

He gazed down at her, fully pinned beneath him, and took in the fire shooting at him from her beautiful eyes, the heightened colour of her cheeks.

'No amount of insults will change anything,' he said roughly. 'Accept it, *agapi mou*. You and I are going to marry.'

After all the lies she'd told, she should repulse him. Yet he was far from being repelled.

He'd spent a whole week with this woman's scent playing to his senses like an orchestra. A whole week fighting his fantasies, fighting his baser instincts.

Now, with her hair fanned out on the sheets like an autumnal cloud, it was like gazing down at the *Venus de Milo*. And as he stared the fire blazing from her eyes suddenly burned in a wholly different manner, her look turning from hate to confusion to desire.

She stilled, her body's only movement her heaving chest.

He *ached* for her.

They were going to marry. There was nothing to stop them acting on their desires. There was no need to fight any longer.

He brought his mouth down at the same moment she

raised her face to his, bringing them together in a mesh of lips and tongues and merging breath.

Their kisses were hard, almost cruel, all pleasure and pain at once. Everything rushed out of him, leaving behind only the desire that had held him in its tightening grip since she'd walked into the palace.

He had no recollection of releasing her hands, but a groan ripped through him when her fingers found his scalp and dug into it, her nails grazing through his hair and scratching down his neck.

There was no slow burn. Every inch of flesh she touched became scorched, and his hunger for her accelerated in a rush of blood that burned. *Everything* burned.

He pulled away to stare at her, taking in the dilation of her pupils and the heightened colour of her cheeks.

He wanted to drown in her.

Touching her, holding her… Whatever deceptions there had been between them, this hunger couldn't be faked.

He straddled her thighs and pulled his shirt over his head, too impatient to bother with the buttons. No sooner had he thrown it to the floor than her hands were flat on his chest, spreading all over him, her touch penetrating through to his veins.

It had been like this on Illya; his desire for her so instantaneous and combustible that one touch had blinded him to everything else. It had turned from nothing to the deepest desire he had ever known.

And that had been nothing compared to the way he felt at this moment.

Had he been naked he would already be buried deep inside her.

From the darkness in Jo's eyes, her short ragged breaths, the way her hands roamed his chest as if she *needed* to touch him, he could tell this desire was just as flammable for her too.

Wordlessly she lifted herself, enough for him to bunch her T-shirt up to her waist and slide it off, just as he'd done once before. As he pulled it free her russet hair fell down with the motion, sprawling over her naked shoulders and spilling out over the breasts he'd spent the past week wishing he could remember with the same clarity he remembered everything else. They were better than anything his imagination could have conjured, the nipples a dark, tempting pink.

She lay down, her smouldering eyes never leaving his face. He swooped in to kiss her again, needing to feel the sweetness of her lips merging with his own. Her arms wrapped tightly around him and her legs bucked, this time not to throw him off but in an attempt to part and wrap around him.

He shifted so the weight of his thighs was no longer trapping her and propped himself up on an elbow to gaze at her.

He couldn't stop himself from staring at her.

He'd never known his heart to beat so hard or so fast.

He ran a hand over the buttery skin of her thigh, which had risen to jut against him, and traced his fingers up over her soft stomach. He spread his hands to cover her breasts, a huge jolt of need coursing through him as he felt the joyous weight of them.

Save for her knickers, she was naked. Her curvaceous figure was every bit as enticing and womanly as the last time he'd lain with her, exuding a soft ripeness begging to be touched and tasted.

Bending his head, he caught a taut nipple in his mouth, felt more jolts bursting through him when he tasted her for himself.

Massaging her with his mouth and fingers, he used his free hand to unbuckle his belt and work off his trousers and underwear. The relief at being released from the confines of their material was immense. All that lay between them now was the cotton of her underwear.

She might not be clad in expensive silky lingerie, but he had never seen a more tempting, beautiful sight.

Joanne…a glorious *Venus de Milo* that only he knew about…

'Have there been many others?' He hauled himself up, the words falling from his tongue too quickly for him to stop them.

Her throat moved, hate suddenly flashing in her eyes. 'You have no right to ask.'

'You're going to be my wife. I have every right.' The thought of another man's eyes seeing her like this, another man's hands touching her…

'And I have every right not to answer.'

Her hand brushed down his stomach to his freed erection, encircling it. Her breaths deepened.

Theseus closed his eyes and counted to three. All thoughts of her with other men disappeared as he gritted his teeth at the delight of her gentle touch. The pressure was light—too light. Torturously light.

He swooped down to claim her mouth for his own. Whatever men there might have been in the intervening years, he would drive them from her mind. He would mark her. He would make her understand with more than words that from this moment on she would be his and only his.

For the rest of her life.

In a swarm of kisses and touches he explored her, trailing his lips over her breasts and stomach, finding a strawberry birthmark as he tugged her underwear down and threw it onto the heap of clothes piled on the floor beside them, discovering a small mole at the top of her thigh… It was all for him. All for his eyes only.

Jo thrashed beneath him, her own hands reaching out and grasping, her nails digging into his back, her hips bucking upwards, inviting his possession. She gasped and cried out when he dipped his head between her legs.

He shuddered with need.

Five years without a woman…

Was it any wonder he felt so desperately on the edge?

But he had felt like this before. Once. With Jo...

He drove the thought from his mind.

He pressed his tongue against her.

Theos, she tasted divine.

She pushed her pelvis into him, her back arching. Her little moans of pleasure were like music to his ears and he increased the friction just a little, enough so that when she grabbed at his head she caught his hair in her hands and clasped it tightly. She was on the brink.

But he didn't want her to come yet. Not this time. He wanted to read her eyes as she cried out with the pleasure of him being inside her. Selfishly, he wanted it all, and he wanted it now, before the craven need in him burst.

Trailing his tongue all the way back up her body, helpless to resist nuzzling into her gorgeous breasts once more, he lay between her parted legs and kissed her, possessing her with his mouth before guiding his erection to the heart of her and sliding into the tight, welcoming heat.

She cried out and stiffened.

'Okay?' he asked, only just able to get the word out.

Her answer was to nip at his cheek with her teeth and wrap her legs around him.

He thrust as deep as he could go, the sensations spreading through him at being fully sheathed inside her making him groan out loud.

Forget savouring the moment—he was long past that point. If he'd ever been there. All he wanted was to lose himself in the incredible feelings rushing through him, to listen to the wanton moans escaping her delicious mouth, and to find the release clamouring inside him.

As he pushed feverishly into her all he knew was that she must have some magical quality he reacted to. That she cast a spell that turned his body into a slave for pleasure.

Her response was as fevered as his own, her arms clasping him so tightly that he lay fully locked inside her, on her, fused with her into one being. Nothing mattered but this heady hunger that had to be satisfied or else they would both fall off the precipice.

Then she broke away from his kisses, pressing her cheek tightly to his own, and her moans deepened as her nails dug painfully—but oh, so pleasurably—into his back. He felt her climax swell within her, thickening around him and then pulling him into the headiness of release. Of surrender.

CHAPTER EIGHT

JO'S EYES FLEW OPEN. Instant wakefulness.

The room was dusky, the early-morning sun making its first peeks through the heavy drapes. The only sound to be heard was the deep, heavy breathing of Theseus in sleep.

She'd awoken to the same sounds on Illya. To the same weight of his arm slung around her waist, the same body pressed into her back, encircling her almost protectively.

It had been nothing but an illusion. However protectively he'd behaved in his sleep he'd sailed away the next morning and never given her another thought…

Everything came back in a flood.

Theseus learning about Toby. His demands of marriage. Making love.

Oh, Lord, what had possessed her?

Where was her pride? Her self-control?

The only crumb of comfort she could take was that whatever mad fever she'd fallen into, Theseus had fallen into it as well.

Flames licked her cheeks as she remembered how willingly she had given herself to him. His caresses and kisses had lit the touch-paper to her desperate, emotion-ridden body.

A tear trickled down her cheek and landed on her pillow. Blinking furiously, she tried her hardest to stop any more from forming but they fell through her lashes, soaking the fabric.

Helpless to stop them, she let the tears fall, wishing with

all her heart that she could turn the clock back a week and tell him about Toby the minute they'd been alone in his office for the first time. The outcome wouldn't be any different—Theseus would still be insisting on marriage, of that she was certain—but *they* would be different. This loathing wouldn't be there.

Making love wouldn't have felt like waging war with their bodies.

She'd never imagined sex could be like that—angry, yet tender, with shining highlights of bliss that had taken her to a place she'd never known existed.

It had been beautiful.

But how could she do it? How could she spend her life with a man who despised her?

Lust was transient. When desire was spent, and without a deeper bond to glue them together, hate and resentment would fill the space, and there was already enough loathing between them to fill a room.

Her parents had once lusted after each other. Her brother Jonathan had been the result of their passion and the reason they had been forced to marry. A decade later, when Jo had been born, their marriage had deteriorated into a union as cold and barren as Siberia. It was a surprise they'd thawed enough to make *her*.

For Jo, having a father who spent his days in an alcoholic stupor and a mother who treated flea-ridden hedgehogs with more compassion than she extended to her husband or daughter had been normal.

As she'd grown up and seen how other families interacted she'd slowly realised it *wasn't* normal.

And so she'd vowed never to be like them, to never treat her husband or any children she might have that way.

Her very worst nightmare was being trapped in a cold, loveless marriage like her parents.

She choked in a breath.

All her dreams were over. The nightmare had come to life.

She would never find love. And love would never find her.

Theseus would never love her. All he wanted was their son. She was the unwanted appendage that came with Toby.

She was trapped.

With fresh tears falling, she shuffled out from under Theseus's arm and rooted around until she found her T-shirt, slipped it back on and stole into the bathroom. She blew her nose, trying desperately to get a grip on herself.

She couldn't fall to pieces. All she could do was try and salvage something from this mess. If she could survive pregnancy and motherhood alone, she could survive anything.

When she stepped back into the bedroom her eyes were drawn straight to him. The dusky light solidified his sleeping form. A lock of black hair had fallen over his cheek. The lines that had etched his face since their return from the club had been smoothed away.

Her heart stuck in her throat. He looked so peaceful.

Hate was an alien emotion to her. Even throughout all the years of her mother's cold indifference she'd never hated her. Neither had she hated her father for his weakness and failure to stand up for her, nor hated her brother for being treated as if he mattered.

She didn't want to hate Theseus. He was the father of her son.

She'd loved him once. To hate him would be to turn all those memories into dust.

As she climbed back into bed, trying hard to keep her movements smooth so as not to wake him, she realised his breathing had quietened.

Pinching the bridge of her nose to stop another batch of tears from falling, she slid under the covers and held herself tightly.

After long minutes of silence, during which she became certain that he was as awake as she was, the words playing in her head finally came out. 'I want to tell you the story of a young woman who graduated from university with her virginity intact.'

She spoke quietly, keeping her eyes trained on the ceiling. She could feel his gaze upon her. If she said it as if she were talking about someone else, maybe she could tell it all without any more tears.

'That young woman had spent her life as the butt of her schoolmates' jokes—mostly on account of the size of her actual butt.'

She laughed quietly, but there was nothing funny about the memory. Jo's only truly happy memories were of that magical time on Illya and the birth of her son.

'She thought university would be different but it wasn't. She made a couple of good friends, but socially she was never accepted. She graduated with her virginity because the only men who had wanted to sleep with her had only tried it on for a bet.'

Theseus jerked, as if recoiling, but she didn't look at him. She had to stay dispassionate or she would fall to pieces, and that was the last thing she wanted. Theseus had enough power over her as it was.

'She had her life mapped out. She was finally leaving the home she'd never felt wanted in and moving to London with her friends. She even had a job lined up. And before she moved into her new life she took her first trip abroad, as a goodbye to her old life. There she met a man—a Greek engineer.'

She laughed again at her naivety.

'One night some men came into the bar and started harassing her. Her Greek crush stepped in and… Well, you know the rest.'

She swallowed and finally turned onto her side to face him. His expression in the half-light was unreadable.

'You were good to me like no one had ever been before. You *included* me. You were *nice* to me. And do you remember when you turned up at my chalet? You were a mess.'

She caught the briefest of flickers in his eyes.

'I'd never been in love before,' she whispered, staring intently at him.

His face was inches from her own, close enough for her to feel the warmth of his breath.

'I hero-worshipped you like you were a sun-kissed idol. And you needed me that night. You made me feel…*necessary*. When you kissed me…it was like a dream. You *wanted* me. That was the best moment of my life. So my lie about being on the pill came out without any thought or regard for the consequences. I didn't want that moment to end so I was stupid and reckless, and I deserve your contempt. I hate that I lied to you, and I will live with it on my conscience for the rest of my life. But even if you never believe anything else, please believe that I was going to tell you about our son and that I'm more sorry than I can ever say.'

He was silent for a long time before he hoisted himself onto an elbow to stare down at her. His eyes were penetrating, as if he were trying to read her.

Jo held her breath as she waited for him to speak.

Instead of saying anything, he turned away and threw off the covers, then swung his legs over to sit on the edge of the bed.

'That night on Illya, I behaved very badly towards you,' he said, his back to her.

'No…'

'I knew you had feelings for me. I took advantage of that.' Now he turned his head. His jaw clenched and he looked at her with hard eyes. 'But those feelings you once had for me…keep them locked away. Never let them return. You know what I expect from a marriage and there will be no place in ours for love. You need to get that in your head *now*.'

He rubbed his palm over his face, then slid his underwear on.

'Any romantic notions you may have—kill them. I will try to be a good husband to you but I will never love you. Protect your heart. Because if you don't it will not only be you who suffers for it but our son.'

She stared at him, the heart he wanted her to protect against him beating so hard that pain shuddered against her ribcage.

He pulled his trousers on, slung his shirt over his shoulder and faced her.

'My parents' marriage was a disaster. If they hadn't died so young they would have likely killed each other anyway. She loved him too much to share him; he loved himself too much and was too spoiled and pampered to deny himself anything he wanted—and that included other women. He would hit my mother for questioning his infidelities and yet, still she loved him. It was a lethal combination and not the kind of marriage I would wish on anyone. I will not have our son exposed to the horrors I witnessed. I will not have him used as a pawn in a game between two adults who should know better.'

He reached the door to the secret passage which led to his apartment and looked at her one last time.

'Just think—you will be a princess, *agapi mou*. That must go some way to mitigating the restrictions you will now face.'

'Like being a prince has in any way mitigated the restrictions *you* live with?' she countered pointedly, a tremor in her voice.

Eyes narrowed, he slowly inclined his head. 'I learned,

and you will learn too—fighting destiny is pointless. Embrace your new life. It's the only way to survive it.'

Knowing there was no chance of falling back to sleep, Theseus took a long shower, hoping the steaming water would do something to soothe the darkness that had dragged him under after his dawn-lit talk with Jo.

He hoped she'd take his warnings to heart.

She was a dreamer like his mother. He'd seen it in her eyes when he'd told her not to fall in love with him and bluntly spelt out that he would never love her.

He had done it the way a cruel child might pick the wings off an injured fly. Except he'd taken no enjoyment in destroying her dreams.

Yes, she'd told him a lie, but listening to her explain how it had been for her had released more memories and he'd found himself feeling sickened. At himself.

He'd *known* she'd had feelings for him and had taken advantage of that because he hadn't been able to cope with his grief alone. He had turned to the one person on the island he'd instinctively known would be able to give him comfort.

But he couldn't forgive her for not telling him of his son sooner. They'd spent a week working closely together and all that time she'd been keeping something life-changing from him. No, that was a deception he would struggle ever to forgive.

Yet he would try. The only way they were going to endure spending the rest of their lives together would be through mutual respect. He needed to find a way to let the anger go, otherwise his bitterness towards her would nullify any respect.

At least making love to her and those few hours of snatched sleep had driven out much of the anger, allowing him to look at the situation with a fresh perspective.

He laughed bitterly. A fresh perspective? In less than

twelve hours his whole life had changed. He'd learned he was a father. And soon—very soon—he would be a husband: a role he'd known was looming but which he had hoped to avoid a little longer…at least until after Helios had married Princess Catalina.

After years of silent dread at the thought of marrying and starting a family it turned out he had a ready-made one. He would laugh at the irony, but his humour had dried up over the past twenty-four hours.

After drying himself and dressing, he splashed cologne on his face and caught sight of his reflection in the mirror. He looked exactly like a man who had managed only two hours' sleep.

He was surprised he'd managed even those. So many thoughts in his head had clamoured for attention, the loudest of which was trying to ensure the news of his son was kept secret for another two weeks. He had a good body of personal staff in his employ, whom he trusted implicitly, but, short of keeping Jo and Toby locked up there was nothing he could do to remove the danger that someone would see them and put two and two together.

God alone knew how his grandfather would react. Would the fact that his most wayward grandson had fathered a child out of wedlock and intended to marry a woman with minimal royal blood be another disappointment to add to the long list?

He closed his eyes, his brain burning as he recalled his grandfather's words when Theseus had finally arrived back on Agon.

He'd gone straight to his grandmother's room, knowing this would be his last goodbye. His grandfather had been alone with her, holding her hand.

He'd looked at him with eyes swimming with tears. 'You're too late.'

Too late?

He'd inched closer to the bed and, his heart in his mouth, had seen the essence which made life had gone.

He'd staggered back, reeling, while his grandfather had pulled himself to his feet and faced him. The King had aged a decade since he'd last seen him.

'How could you not be here for her? She asked for you—many times—but you let her down again. And this time right at the moment she needed you the most. You disappointed her. I'm ashamed to call you my blood.'

It had been five years and still the words were as fresh to Theseus's ears as they'd been back then.

He *wanted* them fresh.

He *needed* to remember how low he'd felt and how sickened he'd been with himself. It was what kept him focused when the walls of the palace threatened to close in on him and the urge in his heart for freedom beat too hard.

A quiet knock on the door that connected his apartment with Jo's brought him out of his painful reverie.

Opening it, he found her standing there, shielding her stomach with her laptop, her eyes wary.

She'd donned a pair of black jeans and a pale blue sweater that hugged her generous curves. Her hair was damp.

'I thought you'd like to be there when I call Toby,' she said, making no move to enter the room.

His pulse raced and a lump formed in his throat.

'I've spoken to my brother and told him what's going on,' she added, pulling a wry face. 'They're expecting me to connect in the next five minutes so I can prepare Toby.'

A blast of dread shot through him.

Theseus had no experience whatsoever with children. How was he supposed to talk to his son? He didn't know the language of four-year-olds.

'I think it's best if you stay off-camera.' She looked unashamedly around his bedroom. 'Let me talk to him.'

He gave a curt nod and led her through to the living area.

'How did your brother take the news?' he asked.

'He was shocked. I don't think any of my family ever expected me to find you.' She shook her head, then flashed him a sly grin. 'I should warn you he's liable to punch you in the face for lying about your identity.'

'He's protective of you?'

'He discovered his protective gene when I had Toby.'

So at least there was one member of her family who acted as they should towards her. In Theseus's world blood looked out for blood, even if someone was in the process of spilling another's blood. That had been what had made his desertion and subsequent failure to be there during his grandmother's final hours so unforgivable.

'What about when you were growing up?' he asked, determined to keep his mind focused and far away from his own past.

'I was the nuisance kid sister, ten years younger than him. He had zero interest in me.'

'There's *ten years* between you?' Theseus thought of the tiny age gaps between him and his brothers, who had all been born in quick succession. It had led to much fighting and sibling rivalry, but it had also given them ready-made playmates—something he felt was an important aspect of a child's life, especially for children unable to form other friendships in their homeland.

'I was an accident,' she said matter-of-factly.

'Talos was a happy accident too,' he mused. 'My parents bred their heir and their spare and then two years later he came along.'

Her eyes flashed with something dark, but her lips moved into a smile. 'I don't think my mother has ever regarded me as a happy accident.'

'Surely you don't mean that?' But then he recalled how

she'd described her parents' marriage and her mother's coldness and knew that she did mean it.

'She never wanted more children. She especially didn't want a girl.'

She must have felt his shock, for she raised a shoulder in a half-shrug.

'My mother is one of four girls. Her sisters are all very girly, which she's very contemptuous of. She has no time for what she considers "frills and fancy". I don't think she actually sees herself as a woman.'

'How does she treat you?'

'My mother is difficult—my relationship with her even more so. Maybe she would have treated me differently if I'd been a boy. Who knows? Still, that's all ancient history. Let's concentrate on Toby and not on my mother.'

Jo took a long, steadying breath and brought her son's face to the front of her mind as a reminder to stay calm. Talking of her mother's contempt towards her did nothing to induce serenity.

Now that she had semi-recovered from the distress she'd felt at Theseus's reaction last night she could appreciate the charms of his apartment, which was a shop of wonders.

While his offices were functional spaces, created for maximum efficiency, his private rooms were a masculine yet homely delight. The huge living space with its high ceilings had dark wood flooring and enormous arched windows, the walls filled with vibrant paintings, ceramics and wooden carvings that had a strong South American vibe—no doubt objects collected on his travels. She remembered him telling her he'd scaled the highest peaks of the Andes and remembered how impressed she'd been. *She* had trouble scaling an anthill.

She placed her laptop on the bureau where only hours before she had been forced into signing the forms which recognised Toby as Theseus's son.

For all his fury towards her, not once had he questioned Toby's paternity. He hadn't even asked to see a photograph as evidence. But then, he'd been too busy laying down the law over his rights as a father to bother with anything so trivial as what his son actually looked like.

Stop it, she chided herself. *You can't judge him for his reaction. You don't walk in his shoes. You knew it wouldn't be easy.*

Whatever Theseus might think of her—and she knew it would be a long time before he forgave her—it seemed not to have crossed his mind that someone else might be the father, and from that she took comfort.

It was the only comfort she *could* take.

She had no idea what the future held, and that terrified her.

How could she keep her heart away from him when they would be sharing a bed and a life together? Making love…

His words of warning against loving him had come at the right time. She'd loved him once. Desperately. She couldn't take that pain again. Especially not now, when he'd categorically told her he would never love her.

She would build on the strength she had gathered over these past few years and make her heart as impenetrable to love as his.

Even if it *did* mean saying goodbye to all her dreams.

Most little girls dreamed of being princesses, but for her it had never been about that. All she'd wanted was someone to love her for who she was.

Had that really been such a big thing to want?

Shaking off the melancholy, she opened her laptop and turned it on. She took a seat and adjusted the screen.

'Do you know what you're going to say?' he asked, standing behind her, close enough for her to smell his freshly showered scent and that gorgeous cologne she could never get enough of.

She jerked her head in a nod and did a test run of the camera. 'You need to stand to my left a bit more to keep out of shot.'

His heart thumping erratically, the palms of his hands damp, Theseus watched as the call rang out from the computer.

It connected almost immediately. The screen went blue, and then suddenly a little face appeared.

'I'm eating my breakfast!' the face said, in a high, chirpy voice.

'Good morning to you too!' Jo laughed.

The face grinned and laughed as a pudgy hand pushed away a lock of black hair that had fallen over his eyes.

Theseus couldn't move. His body was frozen as he gazed at the happy little boy dressed in cartoon pyjamas.

Jo had been right.

No one looking at this child could ever doubt he was a Kalliakis. It was like looking at a living version of his own childhood photographs.

CHAPTER NINE

'I'VE DRAWN YOU another picture,' the boy—Toby—his son—was saying. 'I'll go and get it.'

The screen emptied, then seconds later he reappeared, waving a piece of paper.

'Keep still so I can see it,' Jo chided lightly.

Toby pressed the paper right to the screen.

'Wow, that's an *amazing* dinosaur,' she said.

The picture was dropped and Toby was back. 'Silly Mummy—is not a 'saur,' he said crossly. 'Is a *plane*.'

Theseus covered his mouth to stop the sudden burst of laughter that wanted to escape.

'It's good that you've drawn an aeroplane,' Jo said, clearly holding back her own amusement, 'because guess what?'

'What?'

'*You're* going on an aeroplane.'

'Wow! Am I? When?'

'Today! Two nice men are coming to collect you and you're going to get on an aeroplane with them and come and see Mummy on Agon.'

'What—now? Right now?'

'Lunchtime.'

Toby's eyebrows drew in. Theseus almost laughed again. It was the same face Talos pulled when he was unamused about something.

'Aunty Cathy is making meatballs for lunch,' he said,

as if missing that would be the biggest disappointment of his short life.

'I'm sure they'll let you eat the meatballs before you leave.'

That cheered him up. 'Can I bring my cars?'

'Of course you can.'

'And can I meet the King?'

Finally her voice faltered. 'Let's get you here first, and then we can see about meeting the King.'

'Can I meet your Prince?'

The knuckles of her fists whitened. 'Yes, sweet pea, you can definitely meet the Prince.'

'Have you got me a present yet?'

'Enough with the questions! Finish your breakfast and then go and help Aunty Cathy pack.'

The cute, mischievous face pressed right against the screen, a pair of lips kissed the monitor with a slapping noise and then the screen went blank.

Jo's shoulders rose in a laugh, then she fell quiet.

'*Have* you got him a present?' Theseus asked, breaking the heavy silence that had come over the room.

She shook her head, keeping her gaze fixed on the computer screen. 'I was going to get him something from the museum gift shop when I'd finished the biography.'

Suddenly she seemed to crumple before him, her head sinking into her hands.

'God, what are we going to do about the biography?'

With all that had been going on the biography had completely slipped from his mind.

Theos. Right then all he could see was that little face, so like his own—the child he had helped create.

So many emotions were driving through him, filling him so completely that he felt as if his heart might explode out of his chest.

She staggered to her feet. 'I need to get back to work.'

Her face was white. He could see how much keeping her composure in front of their son had cost her.

'Now?'

'Yes. Now. I need to do something.' Her hands had balled back into fists. 'We're turning his life upside down, ripping him away from everything and everyone he knows—'

'No,' he cut in. 'You can't think of it like that. We're building him a new, *better* life.'

'I *am* trying to think of it like that. I'm trying not to be selfish and not to think of the personal cost. I'm trying not to think that I'm throwing away my future happiness just so you can secure your heir when your heir is happy exactly as he is!'

The colour on her face had risen to match the raising of her voice.

'He will be happy *here*,' he said with authority. He would ensure it. Whatever it took.

But would she…?

'We will work together to make him happy,' he added in a softer tone.

She breathed heavily, then unfurled her fists and gave a long sigh. She nodded almost absently.

He watched her closely to see if she had herself under control.

'The book needs to be finished. Are you sure you can carry on with it?'

Her face twitched and she looked away, biting into her lip. Then she seemed to shake herself and met his gaze. 'Your grandfather is our son's great-grandfather. He is a remarkable man and deserves to have his story told. I will do it for him.'

Those blue-grey eyes held his, and understanding flew between them.

Jo understood.

'But *you'll* need to do the bulk of the childcare when

Toby gets here,' she added, after a beat in which the tension between them had grown thick enough to swim through.

'I know nothing about childcare.'

She laughed, but there was no humour in the sound. 'You're the one insisting on being an instant father. I'll work until he arrives—the distraction will be good for me—but when he gets here… Trust me, there is nothing like an energetic four-year-old to put the brakes on whatever you're supposed to be doing.'

'How much longer do you think you'll need to get it finished?'

'I can make the deadline, but I will need help with Toby for the next few days.'

'I have excellent staff at my home who will happily entertain a child.' He began to think who amongst them would be best placed for the job.

Jo's eyes hardened, then sent him a look he was already starting to recognise—it was the mother tiger preparing to appear.

'You are not turning his life upside down only to palm him off on *staff*,' she said steadily. 'Being a father requires a lot more than marrying the child's mother, giving him a title and writing him into your will.'

His temperature rose at her implied rebuke, but he spoke coolly. 'I know exactly what being a father entails, but it is impossible for me to put all my work and duties to one side without prior planning.'

'Don't lie to me.' Her eyes flashed a warning. 'There have been enough lies between us. Now we draw a line in the sand and tell no more. From now on we speak only the truth. You want Toby here and in your life, so it's up to you to forge a relationship with him. You're the adult, so it must come from you. He's a sociable, gregarious boy and I know that the second he learns you're his father he'll be stuck to your side like glue.'

That was what scared him.

Theseus remembered being a small boy and wanting nothing more than his father's attention. But his father's attention had been wrapped up entirely in his eldest son and heir, Helios. As the spare, Theseus had never been deemed worthy of his father's time, had always been left trailing in Helios's wake.

The favouritism had been blatant, and with only a year between them Theseus had felt the rift deeply. His mother had tried to make up for it, lavishing him with love, but it hadn't been enough. It had been his father's respect and love he had so desired.

What if Toby found him lacking? What if he was as great a disappointment as a father as he had been as a son and a grandson?

He needed time.

His overriding priority was to get his son safely to the island and under his protection. Anything after that…

'I will make the necessary arrangements after I have spoken to Helios,' he said, ignoring her swift intake of breath. 'There is much to arrange, *agapi mou*,' he continued smoothly. 'A prince's wedding on this island is usually a state affair, but I am not prepared to wait for the months of planning that will take. I am going to tell Helios of our plans—I want my ring on your finger as soon as it can be arranged.'

'I thought you were going to keep things a secret until after the Gala?' This time there was no hiding her bitterness. He knew he was railroading her into this marriage, but he also knew it was the best course of action for all of them—especially for Toby.

'Only from my grandfather. Since we've known of his illness Helios has been running things in preparation for when…' He shook his head. She knew when. 'Helios's staff can work with mine to get the preparations up and running.'

'You don't hang around, do you?'

'Not when it comes to important matters, no.'

She rubbed her eyes, then sighed. 'Will Helios want to meet me?'

'For sure. But don't worry about it—he's a good guy.'

'And what about Talos? Will you tell him too?'

'If I can get him to myself for more than a minute. He's working closely with the Gala's solo violinist, and if the rumours are to be believed—which they probably are, as palace gossip here is generally reliable—she's playing more than just her violin for him.'

Jo gave a bark of surprised laughter at his innuendo.

He grinned as the sound lightened his heart. That was better. Seeing Jo laugh was a whole lot better than seeing her cry.

He might not be anywhere near a place of forgiveness, but he was no sadist.

He swallowed down the notion that seeing Jo cry felt like a knife being stabbed in his heart.

The sun had long gone down over Theseus's Mediterranean beachside villa when the driver pulled to a stop outside. Toby had fallen asleep in the car, curled up in her arms. According to Nikos he'd spent the entire flight talking. No wonder he was so exhausted.

But, other than being worn out with all the travel and excitement of the day, Toby had been his usual happy self and overjoyed to be with his mummy.

The butler, a man who looked as if he should be surfing in Hawaii rather than running a prince's household, was there to greet them. Nikos took Toby's suitcase inside, leaving Jo, at her insistence, to carry Toby inside.

She'd packed her clothes and then worked on the biography until the call had come through that the plane was circling above the island. Dimitris had accompanied her to the airport. She'd had no idea where Theseus was; she hadn't seen him since the morning.

Her blood had boiled. She had been totally unable to believe that the man who was turning three lives inside out was failing to meet his own son.

Now, as she followed the butler inside, treading over the cool marble tiles, she wondered if all her work stuff had been brought over as Dimitris had promised. She hoped they'd remembered to bring her suitcase. There were so many things to think of her head was full enough to overspill.

Although not as grand as the palace—how could *any* dwelling possibly compare with that?—Theseus's villa had an eclectic majesty all of its own. The façade a dusky yellow, the interiors were wide and spacious; filled with more of the South American vibe she'd felt in his palace apartment. Bold colours, stunning canvases and statuettes—homely, yet rich. A place she felt immediately at ease in.

It was the kind of vibe she'd always imagined Theo's home would have.

Shivers coiled up her spine.

For all of Theseus's talk that Theo didn't exist, this house proved that he did.

She and Toby had been given rooms opposite each other on the second floor. Toby's was large and airy, with a double bed. His sleepy eyes widened to see it.

'Is that mine?' he asked, yawning.

'While we're here, yes.' Placing him on the bed, she rooted through his suitcase until she found a pair of pyjamas.

'How long are we staying for, Mummy?'

What could she say? He'd only just arrived. Did she have to tell him so soon that their stay here would be for ever and that the life he knew and loved was gone?

She was saved from having to answer by a soft tap on the door. A young woman, no older than twenty, stood at the doorway almost bouncing with excitement. She introduced herself as her maid, Elektra.

'My maid?' Jo asked, puzzled.

'Yes, *despinis*. I am excited to meet you and your son.'

Elektra stepped into the room. When she looked at Toby her eyes widened. 'He has—'

'I need to get Toby settled down for the night,' Jo interrupted, certain the maid was about to make a reference to Toby's likeness to Theseus. 'If you give me ten minutes, then you can show me what's what.'

Understanding flashed in Elektra's eyes. 'I'll unpack your cases. Nice to meet you, Toby.'

When she was alone with her son, Jo got him washed, teeth brushed and into his pyjamas. He was already falling asleep when she kissed him goodnight and slipped from his room, going across the corridor into her own.

She stepped inside on weary feet, but still had enough energy to sigh with pleasure at the room's graceful simplicity and creamy palette. Looking at the four-poster bed, with its inviting plump pillows, she knew she at least had a sanctuary that was all her own. This room was entirely feminine.

Her chest squeezed and she shut her eyes tight, fighting back a sudden batch of tears.

Shouldn't she be happy? She was going to be a princess! Her son would never want for anything ever again. There would be no more juggling money or eking out her salary, no more shame at sending Toby to preschool with trousers an inch too short. As Theseus's son he would have the best of everything, from clothing to education. And so would she, as his wife.

She would never have to struggle again.

She should be as happy as one of her mother's pampered animals.

So why did she feel so heartsick?

* * *

The villa sat in silence when Nikos dropped Theseus off outside the main door.

Philippe, his young, energetic butler, greeted him. After exchanging a few words about the two new members of the household, Theseus dismissed him for the night.

At the palace there were always staff members on shift. If he wanted a three-course meal at three o'clock in the morning, a three-course meal would appear. Always somewhere there would be activity.

Here, in his personal domain, away from stuffy protocol, he liked a more relaxed, informal atmosphere. If he wanted a three-course meal at three o'clock in the morning he would damn well make it himself. Not that he could cook anything other than cheese on toast—a hangover from his English boarding school days and still his favourite evening snack.

Tonight he was too tired to eat.

Dragging himself up the stairs on legs that felt as if they had weights in them, he reached the room his son slept in. He stood at the partly open door for an age before stepping inside.

A night light in the shape of a train had been placed by the bed, giving the room a soft, warm glow. On the bed itself he could see nothing but a tiny bundle, swamped by the outsized proportions of the sheets, fast asleep.

He trod forward silently and reached Toby's side. All that was visible of him in the pile of sheets was a shock of black hair. He stood there for a long time, doing nothing but watching the little bundle's frame rise and fall.

He waited for a feeling of triumph to hit him.

His son was here, sleeping in his home, safe under his protection. But there was no triumph he could discern in the assortment of emotions raging through him, just a swelling of his chest and a tightness in his gut.

He went to lean over and kiss him but stopped. If he woke him it would scare him. In his son's eyes Theseus was a stranger.

Jo's bedroom door opposite was also ajar. A light, fruity scent pervaded the air. He went in and stuck his head around the open en-suite bathroom door.

Jo lay in the sunken bath, her russet hair piled on top of her head, her eyes shut.

She must have sensed his presence for she turned her head, jolted, and sat up quickly, sloshing water everywhere. She folded her arms to cover her breasts and glared at him.

'Sorry—I didn't mean to scare you,' he said, his mood lifting. After feeling as if he could fall asleep standing up, he now felt a burst of energy zing through him at seeing her in all her delicious nakedness. Not that he could see much of her; the bath was filled with so many bubbles he suspected she'd poured in half the bottle of bubble bath.

'Have you never heard of knocking?' she asked crossly.

'The door was open,' he said with a shrug.

She lay down again, still keeping her arms across her breasts. She raised her left thigh and twisted slightly away from him, to keep her modesty. 'I kept the door open so I could hear if Toby woke up.'

He perched on the edge of the bath. 'Does he normally wake?'

'No, but he's been flown here from England to this strange place with hardly any warning—that's got to be unsettling.' Her accusatory glare dared him to contradict her.

'He's fast asleep now,' he pointed out reasonably. He studied her face, taking in the dark shadows under her eyes. 'You look as if you'll be fast asleep soon too.'

'I'm shattered.' Thus saying, she smothered a yawn, although still taking care to cover as much of her breasts as she could.

'It's been a long day,' he agreed, unable to tear his eyes

away from her. Every inch of her was perfect, from the autumn-leaf-coloured hair to the softly curved stomach and shapely legs. She was a treasure trove of womanly delights he was certain had not been shared by many others.

Her cheeks coloured under the weight of his stare. 'Did you speak to Helios?'

'Yes.'

'How did he react?' She looked as if she hoped his brother had put the brakes on their marriage.

'He was shocked.'

An understatement. Helios had looked as if he'd walked into a door. But after he'd got over the shock he'd given his full, enthusiastic backing. Thinking back, there had been something in his brother's manner which had made Theseus think Helios was relieved, but he couldn't for the life of him fathom why.

'He was also in agreement that we should keep it from our grandfather until after the Gala.'

Her eyes narrowed. '*It*? Do you mean *Toby*?'

'I mean the whole situation—Toby and our forthcoming marriage.'

He leaned forward and traced a thumb over her cheekbone. 'The date has been set for a fortnight after the Gala. We marry in four weeks.'

CHAPTER TEN

WITH TINGLES CREEPING along her skin at his touch, Jo swallowed. 'Four weeks? That soon?'

'Yes, *agapi mou*. Helios agrees the sooner the better.'

'But he has his own wedding to arrange. Shouldn't his take precedence?'

His thumb brushed over to dance around her ear. 'His will be a large state affair and will take months to arrange.' His voice thickened. 'Ours will be more intimate. There will have to be some pomp to it, as that is expected, but nothing like his.'

Jo closed her eyes, thinking her head might just spin off.

Four weeks… *Four weeks?*

Who the hell could organise a royal wedding in four weeks? She knew he wanted to get his ring on her finger quickly, but this…

Her eyes flew open as she felt his fingertips trail down her neck to her chest, then dip lower to run gently along the top of her cleavage. He took hold of her arms, still stubbornly covering her breasts, and gently prised them apart, exposing her to him.

'You're beautiful,' he murmured. 'Don't hide yourself from me.'

She sucked in air, willing herself not to respond.

'You're going to be my wife,' he continued, a finger now encircling a nipple. 'And you might already have the cells of a new life growing within you,' he added, reminding her of their failure to use contraception the night before, something that hadn't yet been spoken of.

His hand flattened over her stomach and continued to move lower.

'Think of how much fun we can have while we make another spare for the throne.'

'What a crass thing to… *Ohhh…*' Her head fell back as he reached under the bubbles to rub a finger against her, the pleasure like salve on a wound.

She should tell him to stop. She should be outraged that he would behave so proprietorially, as if her body were his to do with as he liked…

But his touch felt so good, somehow driving out all the angst she'd been carrying. The gentle friction increased and sensation built inside her.

'You're getting wet,' she whispered, struggling to find her voice under this assault on her senses.

His eyes gleamed and dilated, and he increased the pressure a touch. 'So are you.'

His free hand cradled her head, pulling her up to meet his mouth and begin a fresh assault with his lips.

'You are remarkably responsive,' he murmured, moving his mouth across her cheek and burying his face in her neck, then moving down to taste her breast, all the while keeping the pressure of his hand firm.

It was as if he knew her body better than she did—as if he knew exactly what she needed—bringing her to a peak until the pleasure exploded out of her, making her clamp her thighs around his hand and cry out as she gripped his scalp and clung to him.

He kissed her again, riding the shudders rippling through her body, murmuring words that deepened the sensations, until she felt weak and depleted and utterly dazed.

Where had *that* come from?

How was it possible to go from nothing to total bliss in seconds?

Theseus brought her to life, made all the atoms that created her fuse together into a bright ball of ecstasy that stopped her thinking and left her only feeling.

He kissed her one more time. 'On your feet.'

Beyond caring that she was naked, Jo held his hand for support and stood, water and foamy bubbles dripping off her. Immediately she was enveloped in his arms and pressed against his hard chest, his fresh, deeply passionate kisses preventing her legs from falling from under her.

She knew Theseus was strong, but his lifting her out of the bath took away what little was left of her breath. When he stood her on her feet she gazed up at him in wonderment, her heart swelling as she took in the defined angles of his face and the dark, dizzying desire ringing from his eyes.

One touch and she melted like butter for him.

Was it possible that one touch and he melted for her too…?

His white shirt had become transparent with the soaking her wet body had just given it, leaving the dark hairs of his chest vivid, emphasising his deep, potent masculinity.

Theseus caught her look. 'Do you want to take it off?'

She didn't answer, simply flattened her hands over his pecs, delighting in the feel of him.

She worked on his buttons, tugging the shirt open and sliding the sleeves off his muscular arms, gazing greedily at his magnificent torso, the smooth olive skin, the dark hair…

'Damn, you are so sexy,' he muttered, breathing into her hair and pulling her close. His hands raced up and down her back, then moved lower to cup her bottom.

She believed him. She could sense it in the urgency of his words and the rapid beat of his heart reverberating in her ear.

And then she was back in his arms, with his hot mouth

devouring hers, pressing her backwards to the chair in the corner of the room.

Holding her tight, he sat her down, then sank to his knees before her, unfastening the buttons and zipper of his trousers.

'You have no idea what you do to me,' he growled, biting gently into her neck.

Emboldened, she cupped his chin and stared into his liquid eyes. 'It's nothing that you don't do to me.'

Their mouths connected again in a kiss that blew away the last of her coherence. All she could do was feel…and it all felt incredible, every touch scalding her, every kiss marking her. She was losing herself in him.

His arms tightened and pulled her to the edge of the chair, then he guided himself to her and pushed inside her with one long thrust.

She stilled in his arms, closing her eyes as she savoured the feel of him inside her, filling her. When she opened them again he was staring right at her, as if trying to peer into the innermost reaches of her mind.

Their lips came together in the lightest of touches. With his arm still around her, Theseus began to move. Hesitantly at first she moved with him, but soon the last of her inhibitions vanished and she found his rhythm, holding on to him as tightly as she could.

As the speed of his thrusts increased she clung to him, her lips still pressed to his, their breaths merging into one. Dark heat swirled and built between them, until the sensations he'd released in her such a short time ago spilled over again—yet somehow deeper and *fuller*—and she was crying out his name.

She managed to hold on to it, riding the climax until his hands gripped her and he thrust into her one final time.

When the shudders coursing through his great body finally subsided he enveloped her in his arms. With her face buried in his neck, his hands stroking her hair, the strong thud of his heart reverberating through him to her, the moment was as close to bliss as Jo had ever known.

She wanted to cry when he finally disentangled himself.

She couldn't speak. She could hardly think.

What was he *doing* to her?

'You're cold,' he chided, his voice hoarse.

So she was. After the warmth of the bath and the heat of Theseus's body the chill felt particularly acute.

He pulled a large fluffy white towel from the heated towel rack and gently wrapped it around her.

It was such a touching gesture that her heart doubled over, aching with a need she knew could never be fulfilled no matter what beautiful things he did to her body.

'I need to get some sleep,' she muttered, no longer able to look at him.

'We both do,' he agreed. 'But first I need a shower. I'll join you in a few minutes.'

Anxiety fluttered through her. 'You can't sleep *here*,' she said, ignoring the fact that this was Theseus's home and he could sleep wherever he liked.

His eyes narrowed.

'If Toby wakes up and sees you in my bed it will confuse him.'

'He's not used to seeing you with men?' Theseus's question was delivered evenly, but with an undertone she couldn't distinguish.

'No. Never.'

His lips clamped into a tight line before he nodded. 'We're going to spend the rest of our lives together. He will have to get used to us sleeping together.'

'You mean we'll share a bed?'

'It's the only upside of marriage,' he said sardonically, pulling his trousers up. 'We'll have our own separate rooms, but I have no intention of sleeping in a cold bed alone when we can keep each other warm.'

'It's too soon. Toby will need time.'

I'll need time, she almost added. Night after night of being held in his arms, made love to… Where would that leave her already frazzled emotions?

Theseus slipped his shirt back on and fixed her with a hard stare.

'I will allow you to sleep alone for the next couple of nights, so Toby isn't upset in the morning, but from then on we will sleep together. For the avoidance of any doubt: our marriage might not be a love match but it *will* be a real marriage.'

She nodded, her chin jutting up. 'Fine. But just so you know, I snore.'

He shook his head and laughed, killing the dark atmosphere that had been brewing between them. 'I thought you said you didn't want there to be any more lies between us?'

Theseus slept long and deep, but when he awoke he didn't feel refreshed. On the contrary—he felt as if he'd slept through a battle.

Apprehension lay heavily on him. He debated with himself whether to have his breakfast brought to his room but then dismissed the idea. He'd never been scared of anything in his life. Why should he be frightened of a four-year-old boy?

Making his way downstairs, he headed towards the dining room, where voices could be heard.

Swallowing to try and rid himself of the lump in his throat, he entered to find Jo and Toby seated at the table.

They fell silent. Toby's spoon hovered between his cereal bowl and his mouth, his dark brown eyes widening.

Jo placed a hand on his back and shuffled her chair closer to him. 'Toby, this is Theseus.'

'Are you the Prince?' Toby asked, his eyes still as wide as an owl's.

Theseus nodded. That damn lump in his throat was still there.

One of the maids came into the dining room to take his breakfast order. He used the time to collect his thoughts and sit opposite his family.

After his coffee was poured for him the maid bustled off, leaving the three of them alone in the most awkward silence he had ever experienced.

Toby gawped at him as if he'd been taking lessons from a goldfish. 'Do you have a crown?'

'No.' Theseus could not take his eyes off him. He hadn't known children could be so perfectly formed and so damnably cute. 'My grandfather does, though.'

'Is he the King?'

'He is.'

Toby's face screwed up. 'Does he have a flying carpet?'

'I'm sure he would like one,' he said, and laughed, feeling the tension slowly lessen.

'Do *you* have a flying carpet?'

'No, but I *do* have some really fast sports cars I can take you for a drive in.'

Toby pulled a face Theseus recognised as the one which Jo made when she was unimpressed about something.

'If I ever get a flying carpet you'll be the first person I take on it,' Theseus said, ignoring Jo's raised eyebrows.

Now Toby beamed. *'Yes!'*

And just like that his son came to life, peppering him with questions about being a prince, demanding to know if they still kept 'naughty men' in the dungeons and asking if there were any dinosaurs at the palace.

This was *much* easier than Theseus had envisaged.

The knots in his stomach loosened and he relaxed, enjoying the moment for what it was: the first of many meals he would share with his son over the course of the rest of his life.

'Has your mother told you who I am?' he asked when they'd all finished eating and Toby had finally paused for breath.

Jo's eyebrows rose again and she straightened.

'You're a prince!'

'Would *you* like to be a prince?'

Toby contemplated the question, twiddling with the buttons of his pyjamas. 'Would I have to kiss girls?'

Theseus's eyes flickered to Jo. 'Not if you didn't want to.'

'Would I have a flying carpet?'

'No, but you could have horses, and when you're old enough sports cars like mine.'

'I *would* like to be a prince,' Toby said, as if confiding something important. 'But when I'm growed up I want to clean windows on a ladder.'

'You could do both,' Theseus said gravely, fighting to stop his lips from twitching in laughter. 'You see, Toby, you *are* a prince.'

'Mummy says I'm a cheeky monkey.'

'My mummy used to say the same thing to my brother Talos. He was a cheeky monkey when he was a little boy—just like you.'

'I'm not little,' Toby said indignantly, lifting his arm and flexing it to show off his non-existent muscles. 'I'm a big boy. I'm going to big school in September.'

As she relaxed from her previously ramrod-straight position it was obvious Jo was fighting her own laughter. Finally she took pity and stepped in to save him.

'Remember what Mummy told you about having a Greek daddy who was lost?'

Toby nodded.

'Well, Mummy's found him. Theseus is your daddy.'

A look of utmost suspicion crossed his tiny face. 'My daddy's name is Theo—not Theseus.'

'Theo's his nickname,' she said smoothly, although her eyes darted to Theseus with an expression that sliced through his guts.

She really *had* spoken of him to their son…

'Theseus is his real name.'

Toby contemplated him some more. 'You're my daddy?'

'Yes. And because I'm a prince, that means you're a prince too.'

The suspicion vanished, a beaming smile replacing it. 'Does that mean Mummy is a princess?'

'Kind of,' Jo said, taking control again. 'How would you like to spend the day with Theseus? He can tell you all about being a prince. Ask him anything you like—he just *loves* answering questions. And you can explore this brilliant house with him.'

Toby nodded really hard, his eyes like an owl's again.

Theseus felt his own eyes widen too, at the underhand stunt Jo had just pulled, but knew he couldn't say anything to the contrary—not unless he wanted to disappoint his son on their first meeting.

She kissed Toby's cheek and threw Theseus a beatific smile. 'He's not a fussy eater, so ignore him if he tells you he doesn't like carrots. Have fun!'

And with that she left the dining room, leaving Theseus with the miniature version of himself.

Jo turned her head in time to see Theseus step into the room that had been converted into an office for her. He closed the door behind him and folded his arms.

'What?' she asked innocently.

'You are a cruel woman.'

'It was for the greater good. Have you had a good day?'

A half-smile played on his lips. 'It's been something. I've

left Toby in the kitchen with Elektra and the kitchen staff—he's already got them eating out of his hands. They're baking flapjacks for him.'

'Flapjacks are his favourite.'

'He made a point of telling all of us that.'

She sniggered. 'You must be exhausted.'

He nodded. 'Does he ever stop?'

'Stop what? Talking? Or wanting to do things?'

'Both.'

'Nope. I swear he's got rocket fuel in his veins. Still, he sleeps really well—that must be when he recharges his batteries.'

'And he eats so *much*!' He shook his head with incredulity.

'Tell me about it,' she said drily. 'He costs a fortune to feed.' She stretched her back, which had gone stiff after hours hunched over the laptop. 'Other than being worn out, how did you get on?'

'I think he had a nice time.'

'Sorry for coercing you into it,' she said, without an ounce of penitence in her tone.

Theseus brushed a stray lock of hair from his eyes. 'I'm glad you did. I admit I was a little nervous. All I know of children is what I remember from my own childhood, and that was hardly normal.'

'No, I suppose it wasn't,' she said softly, wondering how anyone could have a normal childhood after losing both parents at the age of nine as well as being something akin to a deity in his own country. 'I know being an instant father is going to be hard, but this is what you wanted. All you can do is try your hardest and make the best of it.'

'Is that what you're doing?' he asked, a strange expression on his face.

'That's all I've done since I found out I was pregnant. I will try my hardest to make our marriage work but only because it's best for Toby, and not because you've blackmailed me into it.'

He winced, then nodded sharply. 'That's all I can ask from you.'

'But first we need to get this biography finished. Right now I can't think of anything else.' Well, she could. She just didn't want to…

The words she'd spouted about parenthood had come from the same store of pragmatism that had driven her to move out of her family home when Toby had been three months old and she'd realised that her mother's indifference to her only daughter had extended to her only grandson.

It had been a particularly chilly day, and the manor had been even more draughty than usual. She'd put the heating on. Her mother had promptly turned it off, overriding Jo's protests with a sharp, 'If the child's cold, put another blanket on him.'

In the snap of two fingers Jo had known she had to leave. She'd gone straight into action, borrowing money from her brother to rent a tiny flat from a sympathetic landlady.

She'd refused to dwell on it. Whatever the future held for them, she'd reasoned at the time, it would be better for Toby than living with her parents.

She didn't want her son running up to his grandmother and being met with cold indifference, or thinking that drinking a bottle of whisky a day was normal.

Jo had spent her childhood devouring her mother's cakes, getting fatter and fatter in the process, all in the vain hope of gaining attention—even if only a reprimand for eating too much. She hadn't been worth even that…not even when the school nurse had sent a letter home warning that Jo was dangerously overweight. Her mother had carried on letting her eat as much as she liked. She simply hadn't cared.

Jo would rather have put her head in a vice than put Toby through that.

Much like the time she'd left home, to think of her future now was to feel a weight sink in her stomach and drag her to the floor. Finishing the biography had turned into a godsend. If she kept her mind active and distracted she would survive.

'How have you done today?'

'I'm nearly there. I emailed you an hour ago with the latest chapters.'

'I'll read them after dinner,' he promised. 'We'll be eating at six—does that suit you?'

'That's early for you.'

'I didn't think Toby would last much longer than that. He's been saying he's starving since half an hour after lunch.'

She smiled, unable to believe how deeply that touched her. 'I'll stop now and do some more tonight. If I fuel myself with caffeine there's a good chance I'll get it finished before the sun comes up.'

'Don't kill yourself.'

'It's what I signed up for.'

He inclined his head, his chest rising. 'I'm going to catch up on some work. I'll see you at dinner.'

Dinner itself was a relaxed affair. Toby happily wolfed down the spaghetti bolognaise the chef had made especially for him, but with the threat that tomorrow he would have to learn to eat 'proper' Agon fare.

'Are chicken nuggets from Agon?' he'd asked with total solemnity, to many smothered smiles.

All things considered, however, his son's first day on the island had gone much better than Theseus could have hoped. He'd enjoyed being with him, which he hadn't expected.

Maybe he *could* do this fatherhood thing.

'I have to go to the palace in the morning. I thought I'd borrow my brother's dog and bring him back. We could take him for a walk on the beach,' he said to Toby, who had insisted on sitting next to him, which had filled him with pride.

'Can I go to the palace with you?' he asked hopefully. His face and T-shirt were covered in tomato sauce.

'Not yet. It's too busy there at the moment. I'll take you in a week or two.'

Toby thought about this answer, then darted panicked eyes to his mother. 'Am I still going to Ellie's party on Saturday?'

Now Jo was the one to look panic-stricken. 'I'm sorry, but we're going to have to miss that.'

'But Aunty Cathy's got me a Waspman outfit.'

'I know… I know.'

She inhaled deeply through her nose and smiled at their son, a smile that looked forced to Theseus's eyes.

'We'll do something fun on Saturday to make up for missing it.'

'But I want to go to Ellie's party. You *promised*.'

To Theseus's distress, huge tears pooled in Toby's eyes and rolled down his cheeks, landing on his plate.

He placed a tentative hand on his son's thin shoulder, wanting to give comfort, but Toby shrugged it away and slipped off his chair to run around the table to Jo and throw himself into her arms.

She shoved her chair back and scooped him up, sitting him on her lap so he could bury himself in her softness.

'I want to go home!' Toby sobbed, his tiny frame shaking.

'I know… I know,' she soothed again, stroking his hair.

She met Theseus's gaze. He'd expected to see recrimination in her stare, but all he could see was anguish. She dropped a kiss on Toby's head, saying nothing more, just letting him cry it out.

Only when he'd stopped sobbing and blown his nose did she say, 'How about we ask the chef for some ice cream?'

Toby nodded bravely, but still clung to her.

Theseus remembered the cold days that had followed his return to the palace from his sabbatical. Night after night he'd lain in his bed, in the moonless dark, and had found his thoughts returning over and over to the woman he'd met on Illya. To Jo.

He would have given anything—all his wealth, his royal title, everything he had—to be enfolded in her arms once again and to feel her gentle hands stroke his pain away… just as they were doing now to their son.

The image of her sitting on the beach watching him sail away had haunted him until he'd blotted her from his mind.

'I'll see to it,' he said, getting to his feet and making no mention of the bell that he could ring if he required service. Suddenly he was desperate to get out of the dining room.

He did not want the look of gratitude Jo threw at him. He didn't deserve it. Toby's distress was *his* fault.

As soon as he was out of the room and out of their sight he rubbed at his temples and blew out a breath of air.

He couldn't explain even to himself how agonising he'd found that scene.

CHAPTER ELEVEN

Jo hit 'Send' and threw her head back to gaze at the ceiling.

She'd done it. She'd finished the biography.

Theseus had given her the green light on the chapters she'd completed earlier and she'd forwarded them to her editor in Oxford. All that was left was for Theseus to approve the last two.

Once she'd imagined that she would want to celebrate. Now she felt that any celebration would be more like a wake.

Her work hadn't just opened up the King's life for her, but the lives of his family too. *Theseus's* life. This was a family bound by blood and duty.

When she'd arrived on Agon she'd been too angry at Theseus's deception to understand why he'd lied about his identity. Now she understood.

He'd spent his entire life being scrutinised, having his every waking hour planned for him—whether at home in the palace, at boarding school, or in the armed forces. His life had never been his own to do as he wanted. He really *had* been like a trapped grown lion in a tiny cage.

No wonder he had kicked back. Who could blame him for wanting to experience what most people took for granted?

But now he was a model prince—a model Kalliakis.

She admired him for the way he handled his role, but wondered what it had cost him.

He'd been happy on Illya. Here, it was clear he did his duty but she saw no joy in it for him.

Stretching her back, she listened carefully. Unlike in the palace, where there was always the undercurrent of movement even if it couldn't be heard, the villa lay in silence. If she strained her ears she could hear Toby snoring lightly in his bedroom next door to her makeshift office. After his earlier meltdown she'd worried he would struggle to sleep, but he'd been out for the count within minutes of his head hitting the pillow.

She'd felt so bad for Theseus, who had watched the unfolding scene with something akin to horror. She wished she could ask him what he'd been thinking, but no sooner had their dessert been cleared away than he'd excused himself. Other than his email confirming approval for the earlier chapters she hadn't heard from him.

She'd bathed Toby and put him to bed alone. Theseus hadn't even come to give him a goodnight kiss.

Had that been the moment when the reality of parenthood had hit home and he'd decided that keeping his distance was the way forward? Not having to deal with any of the literal or figurative messy stuff?

Inexplicably, hot tears welled up, gushing out of her in a torrent. She didn't try to hold them back.

She didn't have a clue what she was crying about.

When Theseus returned to the villa from the palace the next day, the beaming smile Toby gave him lightened the weight bearing down on his shoulders.

Toby even jumped down from his seat at the garden table where he and Jo were sitting and ran to him.

It was only when he got close that Theseus realised all of Toby's joy was bound up in Theseus's companion—Helios's black Labrador. It didn't matter. It was good to see him smile after his misery the night before.

'What's his name?' Toby asked, flinging his arms around the dog's neck.

'Benedict.'

Luckily Benedict was the softest dog in the world, and happy to have a four-year-old hurtle into him. His only response was to give Toby a great big lick on the cheek. If Benedict had been a human he would have been a slur on the Kalliakis name, but because he was a dog everyone could love him and fuss over him unimpeded.

'That's a silly name for a dog.'

'I'll be sure to tell my brother that,' he answered drily, not adding that his brother was in fact Toby's uncle. He didn't want to upset him any more, and had no idea what the triggers might be.

'Can we take him for a walk on the beach?'

'Sure. Give me five minutes to change and we can go.'

Throughout this exchange Jo didn't say a word as she leaned over the table, putting in the pieces of what he saw to be a jigsaw.

'Are you going to join us?' he called, certain that she'd been listening.

'I would love to.'

'Five minutes.'

He strolled inside and headed up to his room, changing out of his trousers and shirt into a pair of his favourite cargo shorts and a white T-shirt. When he got back Jo and Toby were waiting for him, bottles of water in hand.

Jo looked pointedly at his feet. 'No shoes?'

'I like to feel the sand on my feet.'

The strangest expression crossed her face. But if she meant to say anything the moment was lost when Toby tugged at her hand.

'Come *on*,' he urged impatiently.

Together they walked out of the garden and down a

rocky trail, with Jo holding Toby's hand tightly until they reached Theseus's private beach.

As soon as his feet hit the sand Toby pulled his socks and trainers off and went chasing after Benedict.

'He seems happier now,' Theseus observed nonchalantly.

His attempt at indifference was met with a wry smile. 'Don't beat yourself up about last night. He was tired.'

'He was also very upset.'

'Tiredness always affects his mood. Don't forget he's in a strange place, with strange people, and a man claiming to be his father…'

'I *am* his father.'

She looked at him. 'He's only ever had a mother. Stories of his father have been, in his head, the same as stories about the tooth fairy. He'll be okay. Children accept change and adapt to it far more easily than we do, but it's unrealistic to expect that to happen immediately. He needs time, that's all. Be patient. He'll come to accept you *and* our new life.'

He wasn't convinced. Did he really want his son to be just *okay*? Childhood was a time of innocence and magic. Break the innocence and the magic evaporated.

Even before his parents' deaths he'd had little innocence left. Having a father who'd made no attempt to disguise his irritation with his second son had had an insidious effect on him. His mother had tried her hardest to make up for it and he'd worshipped her in return. When she'd died it had been as if his whole world had ended. Yet he'd mourned his father too. Loving him and hating him had lived side by side within him. For his mother, though, he had felt only love, and it had been the hole left in his heart by her loss that had cut the most. If not for his grandparents he would have been completely lost. They'd always been there for him.

As he'd read through the final chapters of his grandfather's biography that morning, before heading to the palace, it had played on his mind how much his grandparents had given up for him and his brothers to ensure they had stability. It wasn't just that his grandfather had kept the monarch's crown, but the way his grandparents had enfolded their grandsons in their care.

Given that Helios was heir, it was hardly surprising that Astraeus had taken him under his wing more than he had Theseus or Talos. But Theseus had never felt excluded by it, in the way his father had made him feel excluded. His grandfather was often remote—he was the King after all—and he'd been strict with them all, but growing up Theseus had never doubted his love. And his remoteness had been countered by their grandmother; a loving, generous woman with all the time in the world for him.

Theos, he missed her as much as he missed his mother.

After reading the biography in its entirety, with all the pieces of his research stitched together to create the final picture, he'd understood just how much they'd given up for their grandchildren and for duty. The death of their son and heir had meant the death of their dreams, but they'd risen to the challenge with a grace that left him humbled and aching with regret. It was too late to tell his grandmother how much he loved her and to thank her for all she'd done and all she'd given up.

Toby bounded back to them, waving an enormous stick in his hand. Theseus marvelled at the freedom that came with simply being a child.

Did he really want to take that freedom away from him?

And could he do it to Jo too?

'I've found a stick,' Toby said, coming right up to him and holding it out like an offering.

'Throw it to Benedict and see if he'll catch it.'

''Kay. How will he know what to do?'

'He'll know,' he said, smiling down at him. 'You can always yell *ferto* to him when you throw it—that's the Greek word for fetch.'

'Ferto,' Toby repeated, then ran off, shouting, *'Sas efcharisto,'* over his shoulder.

'Did he just say thank you to me?' he asked, staring at Jo in astonishment, certain that his ears must be blocked with water from his morning swim.

'I've taught him a few words and phrases in Greek,' she conceded.

The admission caught him right in the throat.

He'd become so accustomed to speaking to her in both their languages that he'd taken her fluency in his language for granted. It was a joke amongst Greeks, Cretans and Agonites alike how dismally the British spoke their tongue.

Fate did indeed work in strange ways.

If Jo hadn't been fluent in his language and the only credible person to take over the workings of the biography—

Suddenly he was certain that she hadn't spoken Greek when he'd known her on Illya. Her speech now was practised, but not flawless. She could read the language well, but struggled with the more obscure words. He'd never seen her attempt to write it, but he was sure it would be an area she would have trouble with.

This wasn't a woman who'd been taught his language from a young age.

'When did you learn Greek?'

'When I couldn't find you.' She looked briefly at him, then shifted her focus back to the light pink sand before them, following in Toby's little footsteps. 'I bought some of those audio lessons and spent every night listening to them, and I got Fiona to give me lessons too. She helped me with context and pronunciation.'

'You did all that in five years?'

'Four,' she corrected. 'And now I'm trying to teach Toby too.'

'But why?' His head spun to think of all the hours she must have spent studying, the determination it must have taken…

'I told you before—I wanted to find you. I even started a savings account to pay for me and Toby to go to Athens.'

'How did you think you would find me?' he asked, more harshly than he'd intended. 'Athens is a huge city. It would have been like looking for a specific tile in a mosaic.'

She shrugged. 'I knew it was a long shot, but I'd have tried for Toby's sake.'

'And what did you think would happen if you'd found me?'

'I stopped thinking about that. All the potential consequences were too scary.'

'But you were still going to try?'

Her smile was wan. 'It was the right thing to do. If I hadn't have found you I still could have shown Toby your culture. Or what I *thought* was your culture.'

She cast her eyes a few metres into the distance, to where Toby was splashing at the shoreline.

'No further!' she called to him, before adding to Theseus, 'He can't swim.'

As she joined their son Theseus hung back, watching them.

They were the tightest of units. Seeing them together, he could appreciate how hard it must have been for her to leave Toby behind and come to Agon.

It seemed she'd accepted the job because of the large bonus she'd been offered, which would have meant she'd have been able to take Toby to Greece to find *him*.

If he hadn't believed her before, he did now. With all his heart.

She really had searched for him.

She really had wanted him to be a part of Toby's life.

If fate hadn't brought her to the palace she would never have found him. He would have spent the rest of his life unaware of the miracle that had occurred and he would have had no one to blame but himself.

Jo followed the squeals of delight echoing from the swimming pool with a smile playing on her face.

The sun was bright, the sky was blue—in all it was a glorious day. She'd caught a snippet of the English weather forecast and had given a sly snigger to see her country was expecting torrential downpours and heavy gales.

There could certainly be worse places to be a forced wife than on Agon, she thought wryly.

Toby spotted her first, and waved cheerfully from Theseus's arms.

For his part, Theseus's eyes gleamed to see her, and a knowing look spread over his face when she removed her sarong to reveal the modest bikini she'd bought the day before on a shopping trip with Elektra.

'Sexy,' he growled, for her ears only, when she slipped tentatively down the steps and into the cool water.

She stopped with the water at mid-thigh. 'Inappropriate,' she whispered.

'He's not listening.'

That was true enough. Toby had paddled off in his armbands to the shallow end, to play with the array of water guns, lilos and balls Theseus had bought for him.

'I've never seen you in a bikini before.' Theseus grinned, sitting on the step beside her.

'I was so fat I never dared wear one,' she admitted wistfully. 'Everyone else on Illya had such fabulous figures.'

She still wasn't fully confident displaying her body, but after spending her nights sharing a bed with Theseus and having him revel in her curves, her confidence was increasing by the day.

He tilted his head and stared at her, then reached out a hand to tuck a lock of her hair behind her ear. 'Never feel you aren't good enough, *agapi mou*. Those women on Illya couldn't hold a light to you, whatever size you were. You're beautiful.'

Everything in her contracted—from her toes to her pelvis to the hairs on her head. She couldn't think of a reply; was too stunned that this glorious, gorgeous man could call her beautiful. If she could float she would be sky-high by now…

Theseus didn't care how thin she was. No matter what, he would still desire her.

She giggled.

'What?' he asked, his eyes puzzled.

She clamped a hand over her mouth.

'What?' he demanded to know, playfully pulling her hand away. 'Why are you laughing? Share the joke. I command it!'

But she couldn't. How could she say that his compliment was the most wonderful she'd ever heard?

'Tell me or I'll get you wet,' he threatened, clearly remembering her aversion to water from their time on Illya.

But she could no more stop the laughter that erupted than she could have grown wings.

Theseus was as good as his word.

He got to his feet, scooped her up in his arms, then threw her into the middle of the pool.

She was still laughing when she came up for air.

Preparations for the Gala meant Theseus was caught up at the palace more than he would have liked over the next few days. He made sure always to eat breakfast with his new family, and spent snatches of time with them, but he knew it wasn't enough. Not for him. He wanted them...*close.*

He brushed away the strange word.

Things would change after the Gala, when he would be able to announce their existence to his grandfather and the rest of the world. Jo and Toby would move into the palace then.

Living in his villa was like a holiday for them. The sun shone whilst they played in the pool and built sandcastles on the beach. The magic of it all had caught him too. The memory of last night lay fresh in his mind; taking a moonlit walk with Jo down to the cove, making love to her on the sand and then, when they were replete and naked in each other's arms, gazing up at the stars in peaceable silence.

For the first time he'd stared up at the night sky and not felt the pull to be up there in space. The only pull he'd felt was to the woman in his arms, and he'd rolled her onto her back and made love to her again.

More and more it played on his mind... How was she going to cope with palace life? She'd lived there briefly, but that had been there for a specific purpose, not as a member of the household. She would need time to settle in and then, once they were married in a few weeks, her royal duties would begin.

His good memories from the beach evaporated as he recalled her startled face that morning, when they'd lingered over breakfast. Toby had disappeared into the kitchen to badger the chef into making more flapjacks for him and he'd given her the résumés of the staff he was recommending she interview after the Gala.

She'd looked at him blankly.

'Your private staff,' he'd explained. 'You'll need staff to manage your diary, to do research for you for when we meet with ambassadors and business people. You'll need someone to help with your wardrobe—my grandmother and my mother both had a personal seamstress to make their clothes—and you'll need a private secretary to manage all of them…'

By the time he'd stopped talking she'd looked quite faint. The reality of palace life was clearly not something she was prepared for.

He threw his pen at the wall and swore.

How much guilt could one man carry?

It was late when he returned to the villa. A few members of staff were still up, but Jo and Toby had both gone to bed.

He found Toby fast asleep, lying spread out like a starfish. Theseus padded quietly to him and pulled the covers which had been thrown off back over him, before placing a kiss on his forehead.

With his guts playing havoc inside him, he went into Jo's room, closing the door behind him.

She was sitting up in bed, reading.

'I thought you'd be asleep,' he said.

'So did I.'

He sat on the edge of the bed and reached out to bury a hand in her hair. She shuffled closer and wrapped her arms around him.

'How are things going with the Gala?' she asked softly.

'Like a well-oiled machine. Apart from the soloist Talos found to play our grandmother's final composition…'

'What's wrong with her?'

'Turns out she suffers from severe stage fright.'

'Ah—is *that* why they've been spending so much time together?'

The suggestive tone in her voice made him laugh. He raised one eyebrow. 'Talos says he's *helping* her…'

With that, they both rolled back onto the bed, smothering their sniggers so as not to wake Toby across the hall. Their laughter quickly turned into passion as Jo's hungry lips found his and her robe fell open to showcase her unashamed nakedness…

Time sped away in whirl of sunshine until suddenly it was the eve of the Gala.

Where had the time gone? Jo wondered in amazement.

Theseus had spent the day at the palace and arrived back so late she was dozing off when he slipped into the dark bedroom.

'All done?' she asked, raising her head.

He turned the light on at a low setting. 'All done. The books are en route as we speak.'

A problem with the printers had kept him at the palace long into the night. All week he'd had to work late. The pace had been relentless. She'd found herself missing him, constantly checking her watch and waiting for the time when he would come back to the villa.

'Have you slept?' he asked, unbuttoning his shirt.

'A little.' She sat up, hugging the sheets to her. 'I think there's too much going on in my brain for me to switch off properly.'

'Nervous?'

'Terrified.'

Tomorrow she would meet the King. When the Gala was all over he would be informed about Toby. Their lives would change irrevocably.

'Don't be.'

She sighed. That was easy for *him* to say.

'I spoke to Giles earlier.'

'How was he?'

'Busy.' He slid his trousers off. 'He said to pass on his congratulations for your part in the book.'

She smiled wistfully.

'You never told me you got the job with him by working for free.'

She shrugged. 'I was desperate. I'd had to give up the job I'd originally had lined up in London…'

'Why?'

'I suffered from a condition commonly known as acute morning sickness. I was sick pretty much all the time. I could hardly get out of bed, never mind move to London and start a new job. I ended up being hospitalised for a month. By the time I'd recovered, when I was just over four months pregnant, the job had been given to someone else.'

Stark, stunned silence greeted her news.

'It wasn't all bad,' she said, trying to reassure him. 'I lost a load of weight, and Toby didn't suffer for it.'

'It must have been hell,' he refuted flatly.

'At the time, yes—but Toby was worth it. And I turned into slimline Jo, so that was a bonus.'

'With the way you always refuse cake I assumed you'd dieted.'

'Not initially. Once I got better the temptation was still there, but I stopped myself. I knew things had to change—for my health *and* my emotional wellbeing.' She shook her head and sighed. 'I fell in love with Toby long before he was born, and that was what made me see that I could eat as many of my mother's cakes as possible and she'd *still* never love me. Not as a mother should.'

At his shocked stare, she went on.

'When I was little I was allowed to eat as much cake as I liked. I thought that was how mums showed their love. Looking back, I can see that it was just her way of keeping me quiet. Carrying Toby, feeling him grow inside me… it changed me. I knew I couldn't let her have that kind of power over me any more.'

'And what's your relationship with her like now?'

'Challenging… I pop in every month or so, to make sure Dad's okay. If he's not comatose he's happy to see me.'

'How does Toby get on with them?'

'I never take him. Maybe when he's older…' Her voice trailed off.

'So what *were* you going to do in London?' he asked quietly.

Theseus hadn't intended to open a Pandora's box with his innocuous comment about Giles, but now it was open he needed to know it all.

'I was going to work at a children's book publishing company.' She pushed a lock of hair from her face. 'I loved reading as a child. Anything was possible in the books I read. Good overcame evil. The ugly ducklings became beautiful swans. Anyone could find love. I wanted to work with those books and be a part of the magic.'

And instead she'd ended up working on historical tomes and museum pieces. He could just see her, sitting in her bedroom, forgetting her mother's cruel indifference and her father's love affair with the bottle by burying her head in dreams.

'When I recovered from the morning sickness I went to every publisher I could find in Oxford and offered my services for free until the baby was born—the deal being that if I proved myself they had to consider me when a suitable job came up. Giles took me up on it.'

Theseus shook his head to imagine that he'd once dismissed this woman as 'wallpaper'. She had more tenacity than anyone he'd ever met.

'They say fortune favours the brave,' she continued, 'and it really does. A week after I'd decided I couldn't raise Toby in the toxic atmosphere of Brookes Manor and we'd moved into our own flat, Giles called with the offer of a job as copywriter. It came at just the right time too—I was hours away from starting my first shift as a waitress.'

He smiled, although he felt anything but amused. 'And you were happy there?'

'Gosh, yes. Very happy. The staff are wonderful. I grew to love it.'

Of course she had. She could have wallowed in self-pity at the destruction of her dreams, but instead she had embraced the cards she'd been dealt, just as she would put on a brave smile when she married into his family and became royalty.

He thought of his grandmother, who'd curtailed her performing career when she'd married his grandfather. The difference was his grandmother had been born a princess and been promised to his grandfather from birth. She'd always known that marriage would mean a limit to what she could do with her career.

He thought of his mother. Had *she* ever dreamed of being anything other than Lelantos Kalliakis's wife?

Yes, he thought, remembering the wistful look that had used to come into her eyes when he'd spoken of his naïve childhood plan to become an astronaut. She'd had dreams of something different too. It was the greatest tragedy of his life that he would never know what they had been.

CHAPTER TWELVE

'Do I LOOK all right?' Jo asked, the second Theseus stepped into the room.

The appreciative gleam that came into his eyes gave her the answer.

When he pulled her into his arms and made to kiss her, she turned her cheek. 'You'll smudge my lipstick!' she chided.

'I don't care.'

'Well, *I* do. I've spent over two hours getting ready.'

'And you look spectacular.'

She felt her cheeks flame at his heartfelt compliment and couldn't resist one more glance in the mirror.

Another shopping trip with Elektra had resulted in Jo picking an ivory crêpe dress that dipped in a V at the front and fell to mid-calf. She'd finished the outfit with a wide tan leather belt across her middle and pair of high, braided white leather sandals.

A fortnight ago she wouldn't have dreamed of wearing something that put so much emphasis on her buxom figure—although the height of the sandals elongated her nicely—but Theseus's genuine delight in her curves had given her real confidence. She'd never shown so much cleavage in her life!

Elektra had twisted her hair into an elegant knot and gone to work on her face. The result was a dream. Her eyes had never looked so blue, her lips so...kissable. Yes, the lips she'd always hated for being as plump as her bottom looked *kissable*. She even had defined cheekbones!

Today she was going to meet the King and dozens of other dignitaries as Theseus's guest at a select pre-Gala lunch.

Boxes of the biography had arrived in the early hours, and a dozen members of the palace staff were already organising them for distribution amongst the five thousand Gala attendees.

But first Theseus wanted to present his grandfather with his own copy.

He hadn't said anything but she knew he was apprehensive about his grandfather's reaction, so she was trying hard to smother her terror at the thought of all the important people she would be forced to converse with as an equal and to be bright and cheerful for Theseus, in the hope that it might settle his own silent nerves.

Once the lunch was over they would go to the amphitheatre. Theseus would sit with his family in the royal box and Jo would sit with Toby and Elektra, who was caring for him in the meantime.

After kissing Toby goodbye—and his, 'Wow, Mummy, you look like a princess!' had made her feel ten feet tall—she and Theseus got into the car and were driven to the palace.

It felt strange, coming back to it.

Barely a fortnight had passed since she'd moved into Theseus's villa but it felt like so much longer. It felt as if she was looking at the palace with fresh eyes.

The sun shone high above, its rays beaming down and soaking the palace in glorious sunlight, making the different coloured roofs brighter and all the ornate gothic and mythological statues and frescoes come to life.

When they arrived, entering through Theseus's private entrance, they passed the door of her old apartment. She looked at it with a touch of wistfulness, wondering who the next person to inhabit it would be.

Climbing the stairs, she watched as the carefree man who had slowly re-emerged during her time in his villa put his princely skin back on. She wished with all her heart that she could pull it off him.

Theseus felt no joy as a prince, spending his days at official functions with stuffy dignitaries and being sent abroad to protect and advance his island's interests. There was no time to climb the peaks or stare at the stars.

He needed to be out in the air. He needed to be free.

The man she'd met five years ago had been free and happy. Joy had radiated from him.

Courtiers appeared at their side and Dimitris was with them. In his hand was a hardback book, with a portrait of the King on the cover… It was the biography…

'He's ready for you,' Dimitris murmured.

He had to mean King Astraeus.

This was the moment when he would learn what his grandson had done in his honour. She hoped he'd recognise the incredible effort Theseus had put into it. She hoped the King would be proud.

Theseus turned to Jo. 'A courtier will take you to the stateroom where the guests are meeting for lunch. Wait for me there.'

The strain was huge in his eyes.

'Are you okay?' she asked softly.

He met her gaze. Understanding passed between them.

Theseus brushed a thumb along her cheekbone, resisting the urge to kiss her. Instead he gave a curt nod and left for his grandfather's quarters.

He found him sat in his wheelchair, looking out of a high window, dressed in full regalia, with his dark purple sash tied from shoulder to hip in the same way as Theseus's own. Only his nurse was in attendance.

'You wanted to see me?' his grandfather said, interest on his wizened face.

Taking a deep breath, Theseus crossed the threshold.

He'd prepared a speech for this moment; words which might explain the regret he carried for all the shame and worry he'd put on this great man's shoulders and how this book had been created to honour him.

But the words stuck.

He held the book out to him.

With curiosity on his face, his grandfather took it from him. Wordlessly he placed it on his lap, and with hands that shook he opened it.

After several long minutes during which the only sound in the room was the King's wheezy breathing, his grandfather raised misty eyes to him.

'You did this?'

Theseus bowed his head.

'It is incredible.' His grandfather shook his head, turning the pages slowly. 'When did you do this…? How…? I knew nothing of it.'

'I wanted it to be a surprise.'

'It's not often a secret is kept in this palace,' his grandfather observed, a tremble in his aged voice.

'Loss of limbs may have been threatened…'

Astraeus's laugh turned into a cough, and then the amusement faded. 'This is a wonderful thing you have done for me, and I thank you with all my heart.'

Theseus took a breath. 'I wanted to create something that would show how much you mean to me. I used to be disrespectful, and I brought much dishonour upon you, but I truly am proud to be your grandson.'

His words were met with a shake of the old King's head. 'Theseus, you weren't a bad boy. Rhea always said you were a lost soul.'

At the mention of his grandmother's name Theseus felt his throat close.

'She adored you.'

'I know. I will never forgive myself for not being there—' His voice cracked, guilt filling him all over again.

Astraeus gripped his wrist and tugged him down so they were at eye level. 'The past is over. What you have created here for me…' A tear ran down his cheek. 'Your grandmother would be very proud of you—for this and for how you've turned your life around. You are a credit to the Kalliakis name and I'm proud to call you my grandson.'

The backs of his retinas burning, Theseus closed his eyes, then leaned forward to place a kiss on his grandfather's cheek. But before he could absorb the moment, and his grandfather's words, a knock on the door preceded his brothers strolling into the room.

'Is there a lovefest going on that we weren't invited to?' Helios asked.

Talos snatched the book out of their grandfather's hands and soon all four of them were going through the pictures within, reminiscing with sad amusement, until the King's private secretary announced that it was time for them to greet their guests.

An army of staff bustled around, handing out champagne and fresh juices as the stateroom filled. On an antique table to the left of the door sat a pile of hardback copies of the biography.

'May I?' Jo asked, dazzled.

'Of course.' A courtier handed one to her.

She studied the cover and the back, then flipped through the pages, inhaling the lovely papery scent only a new book emitted.

At the bottom of the front cover were the words *Fiona Samaras & Joanne Brookes.*

She traced her finger over her name, then carefully turned some pages. Pride filled her to know that this was something *she'd* helped create, but with it came a tinge of sadness that Fiona couldn't be there to revel in their accomplishment too. After four years of working together, and all Fiona's Greek tuition, they'd become good friends. Jo knew how much she would have loved to be there today.

While she waited for Theseus to join her she studied the photographs in the biography, which dated back a century, to the King's own parents' marriage. What a family she was moving into…

Where before she'd felt terror at the mere thought of becoming a Kalliakis, she now felt an immense pride and a determination to play her part. She'd grown to love the island, and the fierce but passionate people who inhabited it.

And what a man she was pledging the rest of her life to…

An image floated in her mind of when she had watched him teach Toby to swim in the villa's outdoor pool the day before. She could still hear their laughter. He'd come back from the palace especially. She'd watched them with a heart so full she had wanted to burst. All her fears for Toby had gone. Seeing them together had been like watching two peas in a pod.

Toby loved his father. And Theseus loved him. She could see it in his tenderness towards him. And sometimes when he looked at her she thought she saw the same tenderness directed at *her.*

It gave her hope. Maybe love really *could* grow between them…

Activity at the entrance of the stateroom caught her attention.

An old wizened man in a wheelchair, who nonetheless had the most incredible aura about him, had entered the room. Theseus was at his side, Helios and another man who had to be Talos were with them.

The four of them together looked majestic. But it was only Theseus she had eyes for.

It came to her then in a burst of crystal clear clarity.

She was head over heels in love with him.

She had belonged to him since he'd stood up for her on Illya, and no matter how hard she'd tried to dislodge him from her heart—had convinced herself for years that she'd succeeded—he was nestled in too deep.

She stared at him as if she'd never seen him before, her heart as swollen as the highest river.

She *loved* him.

He came straight to her and took her hand. 'My grandfather wishes to meet you before we go in to lunch.'

There was a lightness to him and his eyes were brighter than she had seen them since her arrival on Agon.

She cleared her throat, almost dumbstruck at what she had finally admitted to herself. 'Do I curtsey?'

'As it's an official function, yes—but only to my grandfather.'

And then she was there before him, this wonderful man who'd sacrificed so much for his glorious island and his magnificent grandsons.

It was with enormous pride that Theseus made the introductions. Jo, pale and shaking, was obviously overcome by the occasion, but she curtseyed gracefully.

His grandfather reached for her hand. 'Thank you,' he rasped, clasping her hand in both his own. 'My book… I will treasure it.'

'It was an honour to be involved,' she said with feeling. 'But Fiona wrote most of it.'

'My grandson tells me you came at short notice and have barely slept?'

'It was all down to Theseus.' She stepped closer to meet his grandfather's gaze properly. 'However many hours

Fiona and I have put into this book, it's nothing compared to the time Theseus spent on the research.'

His grandfather turned his face to him, his eyes brimming. 'Yes. I am a lucky man. I have three fine grandsons—my island is in safe hands.'

Theseus's chest had grown so tight during this exchange it felt bruised. *She was championing him.*

A footman came into the room to announce that lunch was ready to be served. Before they could file out Astraeus caught hold of Theseus's wrist and beckoned him down.

'I am guessing she is the mother of your son?'

His mouth dropped open.

His grandfather gave a laugh. 'Did you think you could keep such a secret from me? A biography is one thing but a child…? I might be on my way to my deathbed, but I am still King.'

'I was going to tell you…'

'I know—after the Gala.' There was no sign of irritation. 'I am disappointed to have heard the news from a third party, but I do understand your reasons. How *is* the boy?'

'Settling in well.'

'I am very much looking forward to meeting him.'

'He is looking forward to meeting you too.'

'Have him brought to me when lunch is finished.'

'He would like that,' Theseus said, imagining Toby's delight at meeting a real-life king. 'Be warned: he's hoping you have a flying carpet.'

Astraeus gave a laugh, which quickly turned into a cough that made Theseus flinch, although he took pains not to show it. His grandfather despised pity.

'I hear he looks like you?' he said, when he'd recovered from his coughing fit.

'Your spies are very reliable,' Theseus said drily.

'That is why they're my spies. You can inherit them when I'm dead.'

Theseus wasn't quick enough to hide his wince. Here was his grandfather, welcoming death with open arms and a smile, and here was Theseus, who would give the flesh from his bones to keep him alive for ever.

'You are planning to marry the mother in a few weeks, I believe?'

'Yes. I apologise for not asking your permission.'

Astraeus waved a frail dismissive hand. 'You have never asked for my permission for anything—why should this be any different?'

'I've *always* asked your blessing.'

'Having already made up your mind,' his grandfather countered, with a twinkle in his eye that made them both laugh. 'Does the mother *want* to marry you?'

'She knows it's the best thing for our son.'

'Don't evade the question, Theseus. Does she want to marry you or not?'

There was a moment when his vocal cords stuck together.

'Do I take your silence as a negative?'

'What alternative do we have? The law forbids Toby from being a part of our family or inheriting my wealth unless we marry.'

The dismissive hand rose again. 'Do you think you are the first member of our family to impregnate a woman out of wedlock? You're wealthy in your own right. There are means, if the will is strong enough.'

'Are you suggesting that I *shouldn't* marry her?' Now he really *was* shocked. He knew how much importance his grandfather placed on matrimony, and how important it was to him to see the family line secured.

'I am suggesting you think in more depth about it before you tie yourself into a marriage neither of you can back away from.' His lined face softened. 'Whatever you choose…know that I will support you. Now, let us meet our guests and enjoy the day.'

Theseus dragged himself off the sofa in his palace apartment, clutching his head with one hand. From the look of the sunlight filtering through the shutters he hadn't closed properly it seemed that the sun had long beaten him awake.

He hadn't intended to stay the night. His plan had been to return to the villa once the official after-Gala party in the palace had finished. But with Talos long gone—chasing after the fabulous violinist who'd brought the entire audience to tears—and their grandfather having already retired, it had been left to him and Helios to play hosts to their distinguished guests.

When the last of the crowds had gone, all abuzz with the news of Helios's engagement to Princess Catalina, which had been announced during the gala, the Princess had flown home with her father and Helios had muttered that he needed a 'proper' drink.

Armed with a bottle of gin and two glasses, they'd hidden away in Helios's apartment and drunk until the small hours. He didn't know which of them had needed it the most. It was the first time Theseus had drunk so much in years.

They should have been celebrating.

Theseus had achieved the one thing he'd set out to do all those years ago, when he'd turned his back on being Theo and embraced who he truly was: he'd made his grandfather proud. The biography had been completed on time and it was a true celebration of the King's life—exactly as Theseus had wanted it to be.

And Helios had just got engaged to be married, so he should have been celebrating too.

Instead, the pair of them had drowned their sorrows.

All Theseus had been able to think about was Jo, and

how animated her face had been when she'd championed him to his grandfather.

No one had ever done that before—spoken so passionately on his behalf. Not since his mother, who would implore his father to treat him as an equal to Helios only to be slapped or, if she was lucky, just ignored for her efforts.

His mother had loved all her children fiercely. He could never have disappointed her, because in her eyes her boys had been perfect and incapable of doing wrong.

Jo loved Toby just as fiercely. Like his mother, she was a good, pure person. She deserved everything that was good in life. She deserved better than him.

He might not have disappointed his mother, but at some time or another he'd let the rest of his family down. When he'd selfishly left the palace to see the world he'd left the fledging business he and his brothers had just formed in their hands.

What a monstrously selfish person he had been.

Even his years of doing his princely duty had been done with the ulterior motive of gaining his family's forgiveness. His heart had never been in it. Indeed, he'd had to shut off his heart to get through it, to be Prince Theseus.

He knew that to make it through the rest of his life he would have to keep it closed. His dreams had to be stuffed away with the memories of his travels before they crowded his head with taunts of what could never be.

'Those people watching the Gala. They have no idea of our sacrifices,' Helios had said, finishing another glass.

It was the first time Theseus had ever heard his brother say something disparaging about being a member of the Kalliakis family, and with hindsight he should have probed his brother about his comment, but his mind had immediately flown to Jo and the sacrifices *she'd* made. The sacrifices she would continue to make for the rest of her life…

She'd been so pale during lunch, and when Toby had

been introduced to his grandfather she'd hung back, her eyes fluttering from Theseus to Toby and back to his grandfather.

Toby hadn't been even slightly overawed, and had happily chattered away as if the King had been a fixture in his life from birth.

But Jo…

His heart lurched.

He knew what he must do.

CHAPTER THIRTEEN

HE FOUND HER in the pool with Toby.

Her lips widened into a huge smile when she saw him. Then a quizzical expression formed as she noticed his set face and the smile dropped. She had learned to read him very well.

Toby had no such intuition. 'Daddy!' he cried. 'Look! Mummy's helping me swim. Come in with us!'

Theseus stiffened.

Daddy?

His son had called him Daddy.

It was the one word he'd been waiting to hear. He'd been content for Toby to call him Theseus, hadn't wanted to upset the apple cart by demanding a title he'd done nothing to earn. Rather like his title of Prince, he mused darkly.

He hadn't been at Toby's birth, and neither had he been there for the first four years of his life. And it was all his own fault for not seeing what his heart had known from the start—that Joanne Brookes was the best person he'd ever met.

And for that reason he had to let her go.

For her, he would cast aside his selfishness and actually do something for the benefit of someone else. To hell with the consequences.

He stepped to the pool's edge and smiled at his son. *I love you, Toby Kalliakis. I will never abandon you. I will always be there for you. Always.*

The words went unsaid.

'Chef is making cookies,' he said to Toby. 'If you get changed, they'll be ready for you to eat.'

'Can I, Mummy?' he asked eagerly, wriggling in Jo's arms.

Her eyes were fixed on Theseus, but she nodded, wading to the edge of the pool and lifting Toby onto it.

Elektra wrapped a towel around him and scooped him up.

Jo's heart shuddered and juddered. Something was badly wrong. She could feel it in her bones.

Please, not his grandfather...

Climbing out of the pool, she reached for her own towel, her heart juddering even more when Theseus made no move to hand it to her.

She wrapped the towel around herself and followed him to the poolside table. A jug of fruit juice and two glasses had been placed on it. He poured them both a glass and pushed Jo's towards her.

'Have you packed your bags yet?' he asked heavily, looking at the jug rather than at her.

'Yes. We're ready to go. Is there a problem with the apartment? It won't be a problem staying here longer. To be honest, Toby and I both love it—'

'There won't be an apartment,' he interrupted. 'Jo, you're going home.'

His words made no sense. 'What are you talking about?'

'Our wedding is off. You and Toby are going back England.'

No. They still made no sense.

'What are you talking about?' she repeated.

He lifted his gaze to meet hers. Unlike the stunned incomprehension that must be clear in her eyes, in his there was nothing. Nothing at all.

'I was wrong to insist on marriage. You conceived a child with Theo the engineer, not Theseus the Prince. None of this was your doing. I'm the one who lied about my identity and made it impossible for you to find me. For me to ask you to give up the rest of your life after all the sacrifices you've already made… I can't do it.' He kneaded his forehead with his knuckles. 'I've caused enough damage. I won't be a party to any more. You deserve the freedom to live your life as you want, not in a way that's dictated and forced on you.'

'Where has *this* come from?' she asked hoarsely. 'I don't understand. Have I done something wrong?'

'No.' He laughed without humour. 'You've done everything right. It's me who's done everything wrong, and now I'm putting it right.'

'But what about Toby?'

'Toby needs to be with *you*. I will recognise him as my son. He can come here for holidays. I'll visit whenever I can. We can video call.'

'You wanted to be a *real* father to him. You can't have a hug with a computer. It isn't the same—it just isn't.' She knew she was gabbling but she couldn't control it. 'Toby needs *you*. Wherever you are is where he'll be happy—whether it's here or in England.

'My wealth is mine to do with as I like while I'm alive.' He dug a hand into his pocket and pulled out a folded envelope. 'Here. It's a cheque. Maintenance for the past five years…for when you had to struggle alone.'

She took it automatically, having hardly heard him. Her head was cold and reeling. She thought she might be sick.

This had to be a joke. It couldn't be anything else.

'I'll buy you a house,' he continued. 'Choose whatever you like, wherever you like. There will be further maintenance too, and I'll make investments and open accounts in Toby's name…'

On and on he went, but his words were just noise.

Panic, the like of which she'd never known—not even

during the night when he'd learned about Toby—clawed at her with talons so deep they cut through to the bone.

'But you wanted Toby to be your heir…' She was clutching at straws, her pride very much smothered in her stark shock. 'If you want to get rid of me we can marry and *then* Toby and I can move back to England. We don't have to live under the same roof unless your constitution demands it.'

He shook his head. 'What if you meet another man and want to marry him?'

'Meet another man?' Now her voice rose to a high pitch. 'How can I *ever* do that? You're the only man—don't you see that? It's only ever been you. I *love* you.'

His face paled and a pulse throbbed at his temple. 'I never asked for your love. I told you to keep your heart closed.'

'Do you think I had a *choice*?' Her whole body shook, fury and anguish and terror all circling inside her, smashing her heart. She wanted to lash out at him so badly, to inflict on him the pain he was wreaking on her.

Theseus jumped to his feet, gripping on to the edge of the table as he leaned over. 'Love does not equate to happiness. My mother loved my father and all he gave her was misery. I can't make you happy. Maybe for a few weeks or a few months—but what then? What happens when you wake one day with a hole of discontent in your stomach so wide that nothing can ever fill it? When the reality of your life hits you and you understand that this is all there is and all there will *ever* be?'

'But *why* is that all there will be?'

And as she shouted the words understanding hit her.

'Haven't you punished yourself enough?' she demanded, lowering her voice. 'You've spent years making amends for the times when you were less than dutiful—do you really have to sacrifice the rest of your life too?'

With lightning-quick reflexes Theseus grabbed the jug

of juice and hurled it. It flew through the air and landed with an enormous splash in the middle of the swimming pool.

She had never seen him so full of fury, not even when he'd learned about Toby.

'Do not speak as if you know anything. My grandparents made more sacrifices than I could make if I lived to be a thousand years old. My grandmother loved me, but I was such a selfish bastard I wasn't even there to say goodbye.'

'What...?'

'I was too late. By the time I got home she'd already died.'

Her hands flew to her cheeks, wretchedness for him—for her—raging through her. He'd been so desperate to get back to her. 'Please...you can't blame yourself for that. You tried...'

'Yes, I can—and I do. If I'd taken my phone with me when I went climbing, Helios would have reached me sooner and I would have had three extra days to get home. Dammit, she was *asking* for me.'

'It wasn't your fault.'

'Wherever the fault lies, the result is the same—I failed her when she needed me. I made a vow that as I failed to honour her in life I would honour her in death, and honour my grandfather in the manner I should have done from when I was old enough to know better. *This* is who I am. It's who I was born to be and who I will be for the rest of my life. I am a prince of Agon, and if we marry you'll be my wife—a princess. All the freedoms you take for granted will be gone. I will not do that to you. I know the cost, and I will not allow you to pay it.'

Loud silence rang out. Even the birds had stopped chirping.

On jelly-like legs, Jo rose. 'There's nothing wrong with wanting your freedom. You can have it still. It doesn't have to be all or nothing. The happiness you had when you travelled the world and the happiness we've shared here, in this villa—'

He cut her off. 'Your time here hasn't been real, you know that. I saw your reaction to the number of staff you'd need to employ, the schedule you'd have to follow. And that's only the beginning. It will swallow you up and spit you out.'

Despite the harshness of his tone, there was something in his eyes that gave her the courage to fight on.

'My feelings for you are real. I'm not a precious flower, ready to wilt at the first sign of pressure. Don't you see? You've made me strong enough to bloom. Meeting you all those years ago… Theo, you made me feel as if I was actually *worth* something. Even here, even during the days when you hated me, you still made me feel like a woman deserving of desire and affection in her own right.'

It was the wrong thing to say. His eyes turned into two black blocks of ice.

His voice was every bit as cold. 'When are you going to understand? I am not Theo. The man you love is dead.'

'No.' She shook her head desperately and gave a last roll of the dice. 'No. Theo's still there. He's a part of you.'

But she might as well have been talking to the leaves on the trees.

'Nikos will be here in a couple of hours to take you to the airport,' he said, turning away from her and heading back to the villa.

No, no, no, no, no. It *couldn't* be over.

But the stiffness in his frame told her that it was.

He stepped through the patio doors without looking back.

Was it possible to hear someone's heart breaking?

Theseus sat with Talos, discussing a new company he'd

discovered that had the potential to be a good investment, but all he could think about was Jo.

He had the impression Talos was only half paying attention too. He'd announced his engagement to his beautiful violinist and it was clear his mind was on how quickly he could get back to her. And Helios had stayed at their meeting for all of five minutes before staggering out, saying he had stuff to do.

Even in the depths of his own misery Theseus could see something was badly wrong with his elder brother. Usually it was Helios who was the sunniest of the three Kalliakis brothers, while Talos normally walked around with a demeanour akin to that of a bear with a sore head. The switch between them would have been startling if Theseus had been able to summon the energy to care.

He'd assumed Jo would be happy to leave, that once it sank in that she had her freedom back she would grab Toby and speed away to the airport, singing, 'Freedom!' at the top of her voice.

She'd been like a wounded animal.

There he'd been, giving her a way out, handing it to her on a plate, and she'd refused to take it. He'd had to force it.

She'd said she *loved* him.

How could she love him? It wasn't possible. He'd done nothing to earn it, nothing to deserve it. He'd lied to her, impregnated her… Yes, she'd lied about being on the pill, but if he'd had his wits about him he would have seen her inexperience and not used her for his own selfish needs. He'd forced her to give up the job she loved, to give up *everything*, and she said she *loved* him?

Theos, he missed her. He missed her sunny smile at breakfast. He missed resting his head on her breasts while she stroked his hair.

'What is wrong with you?' Talos demanded, breaking through his thoughts.

'Nothing.'

'Well, your "nothing" is getting on my nerves.'

'Sorry.'

Talos shook his head with incredulity. 'Get up.'

'What?'

'Get up. You're coming to my gym. You need to work your "nothing" out. You're no good for anything with your head in Oxford.'

Theseus jumped to his feet. 'What would *you* know about it?' he snarled.

Talos folded his arms and fixed him with his stare. 'More than you think.'

Her coffee had gone cold.

Oh, well, it was disgusting anyway.

The coffee Theseus's staff served had ruined her palate for anything else.

At least it was only her taste buds. It wasn't as if the coffee had ruined everything else. No, Theseus had done that all on his own.

She'd been back in England for a week. A whole week. One hundred and sixty-eight interminably long hours, spent doing little other than trying not to wallow in front of Toby.

His preschool had taken him back with open arms so she had a few hours each day in which to bawl and rant and punch pillows. He was a resilient little thing, and his resilience had been helped when her landlady had let them move straight back in as she'd not yet relet their flat.

It was as if they'd never left England in the first place.

Their whole time on Agon might as well have been a dream.

Except no dream would have had her waking with cramping in her chest and awful flu-like symptoms.

She was thankful she'd never told Toby they were moving permanently to Agon. She'd figured it was best to just take things one day at a time. Having achieved his dream of meeting the King—his great-grandfather—and with the promise that he could go back and visit his daddy soon, he'd been happy to return to England and see his friends and his aunt, uncle and cousin.

At a loss for what to do, she stood at the window and looked out over the bustling street below. All those people going somewhere in the miserable spring drizzle.

Pressing her cheek against the cold glass, she closed her eyes.

What was he doing right now? Who was he with?

Did he miss Toby?

Did he miss *her*?

Did he even think about her?

She brushed away another tear, wondering when they would dry up. So many pathetic tears…

She had battled too hard in her life to be a victim.

If Theo didn't love her, then there was nothing she could do about it. All she could do was pull herself up and carry on.

But she felt so cold.

She would give anything to feel some warmth.

Theseus sat in his grandfather's study, ostensibly studying the chessboard while waiting for his grandfather to make his move. Yet his mind was far from the intricately carved black and white pieces before him. It was thousands of miles away. In Oxford. Where it had been for well over a week now.

'Are you going to make your move?'

He blinked rapidly, snapping himself out of the trance he'd fallen into.

His grandfather was staring at him, concern on his aged face.

It was the first game of chess they'd played since the

Gala. Since he'd sent Jo away. He'd made a brief visit to his grandfather to inform him that the engagement was off and that Jo and Toby would be returning to England. He'd braced himself for a barrage of questions but none had come forth. His announcement had been met with a slow nod and the words, 'You're a grown man. You know what's best for you and your family.'

Theseus moved his Bishop, realising too late he'd left his Queen exposed.

'It will get better,' his grandfather said.

Instead of denying that there was anything to improve, Theseus shook his head. 'Will it?'

His grandfather's eyes drilled into him. 'Can it get any worse?'

'No.'

But of course it could get worse. One day Toby—who now had his own phone, on which he could have face-to-face conversations with him at any time he liked—would casually mention a new uncle.

It wouldn't happen soon. Jo wasn't the kind of woman to jump out of one man's bed and straight into another…

He closed his eyes, waiting for the lance of pain imagining her with another man would bring. It didn't come. The picture wouldn't form. His brain simply could not conjure up an image of Jo with someone else.

She'd said there had been no other. She'd been a virgin when she had met him. He remained her only lover.

It suddenly occurred to him that she'd been his last lover too.

There had been no one but her since Illya.

'Do I understand that you finally gave her the choice of whether or not to marry you and she chose the latter?' his grandfather asked, studying the board before them.

Theseus swallowed. 'No. I set her free.'

'Did she want to be set free?'

He paused before answering truthfully, 'No.'

His grandfather's finger rested on his castle. 'You took away her choice in the matter?'

'For her own good.'

The watery eyes sharpened. 'People should make their own choices.'

'Even if they're the wrong ones?'

'I thought your grandmother was the wrong choice for me,' his grandfather said lightly, after a small pause. 'She was born a princess, but I thought her too independent-minded to cope with being a queen. If I'd been given the choice I would have chosen someone else—and that would have been the wrong choice. We complemented each other, despite our differences. She gave me a fresh perspective on life.'

A twinkle came into his grandfather's eyes.

'She understood *your* struggles and helped me to understand them too. She was a queen in every way, and I thanked God every day of our life together that the choice had been taken out of my hands, because I would never have found the love we shared with anyone else.'

Theseus rubbed the nape of his neck, breathing heavily.

There was that word again. *Love.*

He'd loved his parents, but they'd died before he'd had the chance to know them properly. Losing them, especially losing his mother, had smashed his heart into pieces.

He'd loved his grandmother. Her death had smashed the pieces that had been left of his heart.

He looked at his grandfather, spears of pain lancing him at the knowledge that soon he would be gone too.

He thought of Jo—her sweet smiling face, her soft skin, her gentle touch. Her sharp tongue when it came to protecting their son.

Theos, if anything were to happen to her…

It would kill him.

And as this realisation hit him his grandfather slid his Castle to Theseus's Queen and knocked it over.

'Your Queen is the heart of your game both in chess and in life,' his grandfather said quietly. 'Without her by your side your game will be poorer. Without her by your side…' His eyes glistened with a sudden burst of ferocity as he growled, 'Checkmate.'

There was a light knock on the door and then Nikos entered.

'You said to tell you if anything significant occurred.' He handed Theseus a piece of paper and left.

Theseus read it quickly. Then he read it again.

A ray of warmth broke through the chill that had lived in his veins for these past ten days. It trickled through him, lightly at first, then expanded until every single part of him was suffused with it.

CHAPTER FOURTEEN

Jo slipped her brown leather flip-flops off and dangled them from a finger, letting her toes sink into the warm Illyan sand.

She tilted her head back and breathed in the salty scent, feeling the light breeze play on her skin.

She stood there for ages, soaking it all in. There was no rush. No need to be anywhere or do anything.

There was only one place she wanted to visit.

She walked along the shore, the cool lapping waves bouncing over her feet and sinking between her toes, the May sun bright and inviting and heating her skin, driving out the coldness that had been in her bones since she'd left Agon a fortnight ago.

Her time on this island five years ago had been the happiest of her life. On this island she had lost her inhibitions, her virginity and her heart. And, for all the heartache, she wouldn't trade a second of it.

Nothing much had changed in Illya. It was part of a cluster of rocky islands in the Adriatic, and the daily ferry was still the only means of getting to or from the mainland without a yacht, or a canoe and very strong arms. And Marin's Bar was still the only bar on the south of the island.

Really, 'bar' was a loose term for what it was—a large wooden shack with a thatched roof and a kitchen stuck on at the back, surrounded by tiny chalets. Most people who found the island were real travellers, not university graduates like Jo, Jenna and Imogen, who had been there for a cheap couple of weeks in the sunshine.

She supposed one day it would change. Developers would get their tentacles on it. Maybe it would lose its charm. Maybe it wouldn't. Change was often scary, but it didn't have to be bad. She'd gone through a lot of change recently and it had made her stronger.

Soon she was standing at the front of the shack with her heart in her mouth, taking deep, steadying breaths.

No more tears. That was what she'd promised herself. No more. Even if today *was* the day she had been supposed to marry Theseus…

What was she even doing here?

Three days ago she'd dropped Toby off at preschool, then walked back along a busy shopping street. A travel agent's window had been advertising trips to Korcula; another Croatian island.

Three days later and here she was. Back on Illya. Back in the same spot where she'd once watched Theseus play football on the beach with his Scandinavian friends.

The bar was empty, save for a blonde barmaid who greeted her with a friendly smile.

'Is Marin here?' Jo asked. She'd always liked the owner; an aging hippy with a pet Dalmatian that had a habit of falling asleep by customers' feet. She'd lost count of the number of people she'd seen trip over him.

'He's gone out, but he'll be back soon. Can I get you a drink?'

'A lemonade, please.'

While the barmaid poured her drink Jo cast her eyes around. It was pretty much as she remembered it. The walls were covered with photos of the travellers who had passed through—hundreds and hundreds of pictures, crammed in every available bit of space. And the large noticeboard where people could leave messages for friends still hung above the jukebox.

Sipping at her lemonade, she gazed at the pictures, wondering if she would see any familiar faces…

There was one image that rooted her to the spot.

It was a picture of her and Theo, the night after he'd come to her rescue. Their glasses were raised, their cheeks pressed together and they were both poking their tongues out at the camera.

When had that been put up?

She reached out a shaking finger and traced their image. Together their faces formed a heart shape.

A roll of pain gushed through her, so powerful that she had to grip a table for support.

Taking deep breaths, she waited for it to pass. The waves of pain always did, leaving nothing but a constant heavy ache that balled in her chest and pumped around her blood.

'I thought I'd find you here.'

Sending lemonade flying everywhere, Jo spun around to find Theseus standing in the doorway.

She blinked. And blinked again. And again.

He was still there, dressed in a pair of familiar cargo pants and nothing else. His hair was tousled; dark stubble covered his jaw. Wry amusement played on his face, but his eyes…his brown eyes were full of apprehension.

She opened her mouth but nothing came out.

She blinked again, totally uncomprehending.

'What are you doing here?' she croaked eventually.

'Waiting for you.'

'But how…?'

He smiled ruefully. 'You're the mother of my child. You and Toby have had bodyguards watching you since you left Agon. As soon as they told me you'd booked a holiday to Korcula I knew you'd come here.'

He came over to stand beside her.

'I put this up,' he said, putting his finger on their picture and brushing it lightly, just as she'd done minutes before.

'You did?' Her words sounded distant to her ears.

Any second now and she would wake up and still be on the ferry from Korcula, the large Adriatic island an hour's sail away, where she'd left Toby in a family hotel with her brother and sister-in-law.

'I found it last week in a box in my dressing room. When I returned from Illya I put everything to do with my travels in boxes and tried to forget about them. In one of the boxes was my old phone. I got Stieg—do you remember him?—to take that picture of us.' He finally looked at her, a crooked smile on his handsome face. 'There were a lot of pictures of you on that phone. More pictures of you than anyone else. Let me show you.'

He reached into the back pocket of his cargo shorts and pulled out his old phone. He went to his photo gallery and offered it to her. 'See?'

But her hands were shaking too much to take it.

With his warm body pressed against her, Theseus scrolled through the photos of his time on Illya—dozens and dozens and dozens of them. Most of them were of the surf on the north side of the island, or the mountains of the neighbouring islands. Only a few had people in them. Of those she was in over half. Only in two of them was she posing—in the rest he'd captured her unawares.

There was even a picture of her sitting alone on the beach in her swimsuit. She remembered that day. She'd been too embarrassed at the thought of what she'd look like in a wetsuit to surf with him and the others. She'd been scared someone would call her a hippo, and even more scared that Theo would laugh at it.

But now she knew differently. If anyone had insulted her he would have probably flushed their heads down a toilet.

How she wished she'd had the confidence to say to hell with them all and go surfing.

'There's more,' he said quietly, opening his phone's contacts box. 'There. Do you see?'

She nodded. It was all she was capable of.

There was her name. *Jo.* And beneath it was her old mobile number.

'Come,' he said, tugging at her frozen hand. 'Let's go and sit on the beach together.'

In a daze, Jo let him guide her out into the sun.

They sat on the deserted beach and Theseus leaned back on his elbows. Jo sat forward, hugging her knees and watching the sailing boats in the distance.

Had she fallen into a dream?

'Why do you think I remembered you had royal blood in your veins?' he asked quietly.

'Because you remember everything,' she whispered.

From out of the corner of her eye she saw him shake his head.

'I have a good memory, but when it comes to *you* I remember everything. I remember standing on the ferry and pressing "delete" on your number. But when I got the message asking if I wanted to carry on with the action I cancelled it. I couldn't do it. When I got home…'

He sat up and grabbed her hand, pulling it to his mouth. It wasn't a kiss. It was a brush of his lips and a warm breath of his air that sent tingles of sensation scurrying through her.

Dear God, he really was here. Theseus was *here*.

And just like that the stupor left her and her heart kickstarted in thunderous jolts.

His eyes were dark and intense. 'Helios has always known he will one day be king. His destiny is carved in stone. My own destiny was to be nothing more than his shadow—his spare—but I wanted something so much more. I craved freedom. I wanted to play with other children and run free.' He pointed to the cobalt sky. 'I wanted to be up there in the stars. But I was born to be a prince. After my parents died I kept thinking, *Is this it?*, and I struggled endlessly to reconcile myself with my destiny, never realising that to my family it was like I was spitting on the Kalliakis name.

'When I was too late to say goodbye to my grandmother, and I saw the depth of my grandfather's pain, I knew I had a choice to either be a real part of my family or leave it for ever. So I put everything about my time exploring the world into boxes, taped them up and put them away. All my memories. I packed Theo into that box. I couldn't be that man *and* be the Prince I had to be.'

He swallowed.

'I wanted to make amends to my grandmother's memory and prove to my grandfather that I *am* proud to be a Kalliakis. I'd spent thirty years pursuing my own pleasure and it was time to grow up and be the man he'd raised me to be. I threw myself into palace life and the Kalliakis business with my brothers. I was determined to prove myself. But inside I was empty. And then you walked back into my life.'

He reached to brush a thumb down her cheek, a wan smile playing on his lips.

'If you'd told me a month ago that I'd fallen in love with a woman I slept with once five years ago I would have said you were mad. But that's the truth. You were there to catch me when I was at my lowest point and you caught my heart. It's been yours ever since that night. There hasn't been another, and only now do I know why—it's because I've belonged to you heart, body and soul since the night we conceived Toby. You came back into my life and the emptiness disappeared. But I didn't see it until I sent you away and the hole was ripped open again. Don't speak,' he urged when she parted her lips. 'I *know* you love me. I've always known. Just answer me this. When I sent you back to England it was so you could have your freedom. I was so high and mighty, thinking that I was doing the right thing, that I took away your freedom to make a choice.'

'My choice would be you,' she said immediately, before he could ask.

'But—'

This time Jo placed her finger to his lips. 'Your turn to keep quiet. I've never craved to see the stars. All I've ever wanted was to find a place where I belong, and I've found that with you. You make me whole. You make me proud to live in my skin. And that's the greatest gift you could ever have given me.'

She traced her fingers across his jaw, finally able to believe that this was real—that he had come to her, had met her back in the place where it had all started between them.

'Palace life doesn't frighten me the way you think it should, and as long as you're by my side I will adapt. I will be proud to be your princess and to represent the greatest family on this planet.'

He sighed and pressed a light kiss to her mouth. 'After the way I treated you I didn't dare to presume...'

'Freedom comes in many forms,' she said gently. 'You don't have to hide the essence of yourself away for ever.'

'I know that now. My grandmother was a strong, warm-hearted woman—she would have forgiven me. Now it's time to forgive myself.'

The look he gave her warmed her right down to the marrow of her bones.

'It's strange, but when I'm with you all my craving for freedom disappears. *You* make me feel free. You bring sunshine into my life and I swear I will never let you or Toby go again.'

She cupped his cheeks in her hands. His skin felt so warm. 'I will love you for ever.'

'And I will love *you* for ever.'

His hands dived into her hair and then his mouth came crashing onto hers.

It hadn't been a kiss, Jo thought a few hours later, when they were entangled in the sheets of the bed in the cabin where they'd first made love five years before. It had been more like the breath of life. It had been filled with promises for the future, something that bound them together for ever.

'Where are you going?' she asked when he slid off the bed.

He grinned and dug his hands into his shorts pocket. He pulled out the penknife he carried everywhere.

He climbed back onto the bed and placed the blade on the wooden wall. He etched the letters 'TK' and 'JB' into the wood.

'There,' he decreed in his most regal voice, snapping the blade shut and dropping it onto the floor. 'It's official. You and me—together for ever.'

EPILOGUE

'GOOD MORNING, PRINCESS.'

Jo opened a bleary eye and found her husband sitting on the edge of the bed beside her.

She smiled and yawned. 'What time is it?'

'Six o'clock.'

'It's the middle of the night.' And, considering they'd spent most of the night making love, she was shattered.

He laughed and ruffled her hair.

'The surf's up.'

That woke her up.

Theseus had insisted on giving her surfing lessons, and she'd been thrilled to discover that she wasn't completely awful at it. Now, three months after their wedding, they loved nothing more than leaving their villa early, when surf conditions were right, and spending the morning with Toby in the sea and on the beach before heading off to the palace to undertake their royal engagements. As per their instructions to their respective private secretaries, their mornings were always kept clear.

Yes, it had all worked out beautifully. With the family's blessing they had decided to make the villa their main dwelling. They used their apartment in the palace when it was convenient, but to all intents and purposes the villa was their home.

Theseus was staring at her expectantly.

'I think it might be a good idea for me to give it a miss today,' she said, her heart thumping at the thought of the news she was about to share with him; a secret she'd been hugging to herself for almost a week.

'Oh?' He cocked an eyebrow. 'Are you not feeling well?'

'I'm feeling fine. Fantastic. I just think it would be wise to get a doctor's advice before I go surfing over the next seven or eight months.'

She giggled when his mouth dropped open.

It was good few moments before comprehension spread over his features. 'You're not…?'

She couldn't stop the beam widening over her face. 'I'm over a week late…' She'd noticed her breasts growing tender, but it had been her stomach turning over at the scent of the barbecued spare ribs they'd had for dinner two nights before that had decided it for her.

'I'm going to be a father again?'

'There's only one way to find out.'

Jumping out of bed, she hurried into her dressing room and pulled a pregnancy test out of the chest of drawers. She'd got Elektra, whom she trusted implicitly, to buy it for her the day before. With Theseus hovering outside the bathroom, she did the necessary.

Three minutes later, buzzing with excitement, she poked her head out of the door.

'What do you want? A boy or a girl?'

The dazed look on his face evaporated. With a whoop, Theseus lifted her into his arms and carried her back to bed.

* * * * *

If you enjoyed this book look out for the stunning conclusion of THE KALLIAKIS CROWN:
HELIOS CROWNS HIS MISTRESS
coming next month.
And if you missed where it all started, look for the first instalment of this fabulous trilogy:
TALOS CLAIMS HIS VIRGIN

MILLS & BOON®

Man of the Year

Our winning cover star will be revealed next month!

Don't miss out on your copy
– order from millsandboon.co.uk

Read more about Man of the Year 2016 at

www.millsandboon.co.uk/moty2016

Have you been following our
Man of the Year 2016 campaign?
#MOTY2016